MURDER ON THE HOME TOUR

◇

Ginny Barnes

www.cactuswrenbooks.weebly.com

cactus wren books
Copyright ©2025 by Virginia Barnes
ISBN 979-8-218-61572-7

Fellow, come from the throng; look upon Caesar …. Speak once again.
Beware the ides of March.
He is a dreamer. Let us leave him.

William Shakespeare
The Tragedy of Julius Caesar

To Sandi and Jay
for all your encouragement, support and help

CHAPTER ONE

George and Cece Coors stood in front of a palatial mansion. High columns soared up to support a massive porch shielding an enormous carved front door. Greek statues spouted arcs of water onto rotund nymphs and cherubs frolicking below in frozen marble splendor.

"It's just like Santucci to inflict the neighborhood with this monstrosity," growled George, swiping a hand across his very scowling forehead. "Who could design such an abomination?"

"Right!" breathed Cece. "Pretty ugly."

"I could see it maybe in Paradise Valley or the Biltmore, but not here. I don't know what's going on with the historical preservation people."

"Heidi calls it Mar-a-Lago on the Circle. Nobody seems to know how it got approved," Cece added a bit snidely. "But whatever. It's going to be on the home tour tomorrow. I guess the home tour board felt there was a lot of curiosity about it. Bring in more people for the tour."

Before George could answer, his attention was turned to a woman outfitted in bright yellow rounding the corner and heading in their direction.

"What have we here?" George's eyebrows arched almost as high as the snow white hair falling over his wrinkled forehead. His eyes made a quick survey of the costumed woman wearing a neon yellow low-cut sundress. Her peroxide blonde curls bounced around long yellow feathered ear drops that looked like exploded canaries. The feathers layered down to sweep across very prominent breasts barely covered by the bodice of her dress. A large yellow purse hung over her arm and yellow sandals were laced up to her knees, gladiator style.

"Hi y'all, " she called cheerily, chomping down on a wad of gum that rolled across her tongue and disappeared behind a wide red-lipped smile. She reached their side and nodded toward the house they had been looking at. "You like the house?" She tipped her head in its direction just as the front door opened and a dark-haired, stubbly-faced man of sixty or so stomped out.

"Dahlia! What the hell are you doing here? I've had enough of your stalking," he yelled at the startled group.

Cece glanced at Dahlia just in time to see a rosy hue rising up her neck to her cheeks. A look of pure hatred flashed across her eyes.

"Ha," Dahlia laughed, waving a yellow nail-painted hand in his direction as if swatting at a swarm of flies. Her expression had quickly transformed to a smirk and a smile. "I'll be here tomorrow for the tour, Sal. Can't wait to see if your taste has improved."

She turned to George and Cece in an ostentatious show of ignoring the fuming man tromping off the porch. "I'm Dahlia, as you heard. He's my ex, Sal Santucci. Such an awful man. Glad to get rid of him. So who are you all?" Her now sunny smile beamed at them.

Cece and George introduced themselves. "And this is Nicky." Cece pointed down to their miniature schnauzer.

Dahlia leaned down to pat Nicky's head, exposing an eyeful of cleavage. Nicky sniffed at the yellow painted toenail that appeared before his nose and flattened his ears.

"So you're going on the tour tomorrow?" Cece queried, trying to make polite conversation in spite of the very angry looking man striding toward them across his lawn.

Dahlia righted herself, brushing down the yellow folds of her skirt. "Yes, I want to see what he built over the ashes of my mother's home. So," she turned abruptly to George, sidling up closer, her large purse swinging around and banging Cece's leg, "what do *you* make of his house?" she asked, looking intently at George.

"I'm an architect," George muttered, shifting back on his heels as Dahlia pressed closer. "It's not my style."

"Ohhh, an architect. How wonderful!" She leaned forward even closer as Cece's eyes widened in amazement. Dahlia's back now blocked Cece's view, causing her to take a step to the side. "I just lo-o-ove architecture. I was going to study it myself," she drawled with a little rueful smile, batting her long bright blue eyelashes, "but the theatre drew me in first. What *could* I do? You just have to go where your best talents are, I always say."

"I bet," Cece muttered, just as Nicky pulled away from her and onto the lawn. Before she could stop him, he was circling in anticipation of a big doggy poop.

"I'm calling the cops on you," Santucci yelled, waving his fist in Dahlia's direction. His red-tinted dark hair fringed over a receding hairline and his jowly face scrunched in anger. Suddenly wrenching his eyes from Dahlia, he saw Nicky for the first time.

"Get that mutt off my property!" he growled, advancing toward them with a look of sheer fury.

"Must go. Bye, bye." Dahlia stepped back quickly and spun around leaving Cece and George to confront whatever was coming from the very angry man just before them.

"Watch your step," Cece warned, not in time as that very angry man's foot skidded forward. "Wait!" But it was too late.

"Oh dear!" All she could do at that point was quickly stoop low and scoop up the tidy pile that Nicky had just delivered, jostling it quickly into the doggie bag. "I'm so sorry but he's not known for his refined bathroom habits." She tilted her chin just enough to look directly into Santucci's bloodshot eyes and added with a little smile and a slight sniff. "Nicky's hardly a mutt. I think you've hurt his feelings." Maybe a little humor to smooth things over? she wondered.

Coming to the rescue, George reached out to Santucci with a hand, "So glad to meet you. I'm George Coors and this is my wife Cece. I believe my brother Ross knew you at West High."

Santucci looked up at George, offering only an icy stare and no response. Ignoring the proffered hand, he backed up several steps, swiping his shoe against the grass. Then he turned his back and stomped toward his garish mansion without a backward glance.

George and Cece silently watched him go, wide-eyed with surprise. "Wow, talk about a brush-off," George mumbled.

"Doesn't want to be buddies with us, I'd guess," Cece chuckled with a shake of her short red bob. "Guess we're not his type. Thank heavens for that."

"What do you mean?" George looked at Cece suspiciously. "What type would that be?"

"For one thing he owns a strip club franchise, I hear. Pretty obvious what kind of people he would like. Hardly us," she said. She was well aware of the rumors that had been swirling around Sal Santucci ever since he acquired a building permit from the city during the time the regular inspector had taken a leave. The result of that permit was the monstrosity before them. Everyone in the neighborhood had watched the construction proceed in amazement. And now, here it was!

"Who cares about him anyway. Let's go, George. I'm getting hungry. Come on, Nicky. No stalling for more time."

For a moment longer they stared at the door now slammed shut.

"A strip club, you say? Maybe I should get to know him better," George said with an innocent little smile.

"Ha, ha!" Cece punched him in the arm playfully. "You bad boy!"

"Yeah, this bad boy needs sustenance. I believe it's lunchtime so let's get out of here." They turned back in the direction of their house.

Looking back for a last look at the departing Dahlia, Cece sighed. What on earth was going on between those two? Santucci and Dahlia. What a troubling relationship. Cece pulled Nicky along on the leash. Nicky always resisted turning around to head for home. So many sniffs and smells yet to meet. A cornucopia of input from all the dogs in the neighborhood. And even, unfortunately, a few cats! How could he resist? But Cece and George were having none of it and so they retreated back the way they had come, pulling a reluctant Nicky behind them.

They rounded the last curve of the Palmcroft Way circle to their small 1930's cottage set back a little from the street by a grassy flower lined lawn. Cece did love this little house and was glad George had talked her into moving into his old childhood neighborhood. It wasn't Paradise Valley or Arcadia but it was so much more neighborly and to her way of thinking much prettier.

"Hey, Heidi," she called out, seeing her across-the-street neighbor heading their way. "Guess who we ran into? The Merchant of Smut himself and he met Nicky just after our little guy left a *presente* on his grass."

"What on earth are you talking about?" Heidi queried. Cece explained their encounter with Santucci.

"Nicky. He pooped on Sal Santucci's lawn right in front of the old guy himself and," she stifled a giggle, "I think he might have stepped in just a tad bit of it."

Heidi couldn't help but laugh at that image but then added thoughtfully, "I'm not sure you want him for an enemy. You'd better be careful around him."

Cece's eyes widened. "So sorry but you'd better tell that to Nicky. It's not like I tell him when or where to do his business."

"I'm going to sit down, ladies," George interrupted and strode onto the patio to deposit himself into a lawn chair with a slight harrumph. "I'm supposed to be taking it easy, doctor's orders," he muttered half to himself since the ladies were no longer listening.

"You know, George knew about Santucci's family when he was growing up here in the sixties and seventies. Everyone said they were Mafia. But he's not so sure."

"Really? Well, that's pretty interesting. I've seen him. He certainly looks the stereotype. He actually greeted me when I walked by his house the other day. And his voice was weird, very gravelly."

George was sitting on a patio chair, rubbing his stubbly chin. He watched his wife and her friend chat, overhearing much of their conversation. He was fond of Heidi, his wife's new buddy in the neighborhood and another member of their newly formed book club. He was glad she'd found a friend. "Come over and sit down and I'll tell you what I know," he called to them.

Cece and Heidi walked onto the patio, settled into chairs and looked at George in anticipation.

"Okay. Here's what I remember. I think Sal dropped out of West High. He was younger than me so I didn't have much reason to keep up after I left home. My younger brother was closer to his age. I'll have to ask him about Sal next time we talk. And if I remember right that gnarly voice was because it was said his tongue was cut out. For ratting someone out I suppose. At least that's the story. A story I heard recently," he added. "Don't think he had that in high school but I could be wrong."

"Jeez! Should'a known that before I volunteered to sit in his house during the tour. Why didn't you tell me that?" Cece's eyebrows arched in concern.

"Honestly, I had forgotten about it. Like I said, he was in my brother's class and we never paid much attention to the younger kids. But," he added after a thoughtful moment, "I think he was bullied. Not sure why he dropped out of West High. The whole Mafia thing was probably a joke. Actually I think his grandparents were recruited to come to Arizona when the Roosevelt Dam was built. Years ago. They were likely stone masons from Italy or Sicily. But calling him Mafia was more fun and Santucci was short and pudgy faced so it was an excuse to call him Babyface like he was not very macho. I kind of remember his face turning bright red in response to that taunt. Maybe that explains his not very pleasant personality. Plus there actually was a supposed Mafia murder of a family in the neighborhood in the fifties."

"I thought the Mafia was in Tucson in those days," Heidi interrupted.

"Right, they were. But here too apparently. The murder was a big deal because the husband and wife lived in Encanto but he worked in Vegas and drove between there and Phoenix. The husband and wife were both murdered here in their house but no one seemed to know exactly what he did in Vegas or why he was murdered. Or who did it."

"That's pretty disgusting. So the murderer could have been living here. Or maybe they came here from Vegas to commit the murder. Brrrrr," Heidi shuddered momentarily but brightened up. "Listen, I'd love to hear more but I'll have to save it for later. I gotta go, guys." Heidi got up to leave. She turned back and waved. "See you at the dinner tonight, Cece."

Cece waved goodbye. She patted George on the arm and smiled. "Mafia or not I'm going to be volunteering in his house in whatever room I get assigned. Maybe I'll have some time to poke around, see if I see anything suspicious."

"Oh, no you don't!" George exclaimed. "I would keep out of his business. You start getting nosy and no doubt I'll have to bail you out of whatever mess you've made."

"Humph, thanks for the vote of confidence. As you know, all the volunteers are meeting this afternoon at the Elliot's house for our own preview of the houses. We'll be too busy tomorrow with our tour duties to see the other houses. So I won't have much time to get into any mischief. But I can ask around. There're a lot of volunteers that have lived in the neighborhood a long time. Remember we're having the thank-you dinner tonight at that Encanto house on Monte Vista. Our quick preview of the homes on the tour is first. Then the dinner, so you're on your own for dinner tonight. Volunteers only. But now I'm curious about Santucci, so I'm going to ask around."

George groaned.

CHAPTER TWO

The volunteer thank-you dinner started at five. The setting sun shimmered across the grassy back lawn crowded with tables and chairs for the dinner guests. Large mesquite trees edged the yard sparkling with fairy lights.

"What a gorgeous yard!" Cece swept a freckled arm around the spacious backyard full of the volunteers for the next day's tour. The Postino's catering van was parked in the driveway with a line still spiraling into the alley. Cece and Heidi were lucky to get there early so they were just finishing off their meal. "But what about our new neighbor where I'll be guarding? What do you know about him? Come on, Heidi. Tell me all the juicy gossip."

"Ok, ok. There's a lot of gossip, of course. I have heard some stuff. See that woman at three o'clock next to the palo verde tree. That's the infamous Dahlia. Former stripper at Club Santucci Scottsdale."

"Oh, I didn't get a chance to tell you earlier. We met her this morning when we had our little incident in Santucci's front yard. With Nicky, you know. I didn't know she was a stripper. Wow, a stripper. Are they still called that?"

"I don't know. Exotic dancer, maybe."

"Woman experiencing no clothes?" Cece suggested, eyebrows raised.

"Woman experiencing clotheslessness!"

"Better!" They both laughed.

"When we ran into her this morning in front of Santucci's house, she didn't say anything about being a stripper. Not surprising. She said she was 'in theatre'. A euphemism, I guess. Obviously, former stripper. She looks way too long in the tooth to be a stripper now despite her, err, *decolletage* showing even over to here." Cece rolled her eyes and looked at Heidi head atilt. "So she lives here?"

"No, she's crashing the dinner as usual. She lives in Story south of McDowell but her mother owned half the lot where Santucci's mansion now stands. The story is her mother died and left Dahlia her house after Dahlia left the Santucci's Scottsdale club. Dahlia had lived in Vegas, working in one of Santucci's clubs. When he opened the Scottsdale place she moved to Phoenix too. He had some kind of affair with her after he bought the house next door to Dahlia's mother's house and talked Dahlia into giving him the old house of her mother's. She told everyone they were engaged and he was going to build a house for the two of them. Well, he tore down both houses and built his mansion alright. Just that he forgot about the marriage part. Said he paid her cash in a private deal and he owes her nothing. She's been trying to sue him for breach of contract ever since but of course there was no contract. She claims his word is a contract but against him and his money that's going nowhere and never will. So now she just tells everyone she broke up with him because he isn't her type and she doesn't like him."

"Saving face, I guess. That must have been hard. To lose her mother's house and end up with nothing is awful," Heidi said softly, shrugging her shoulders. "I'll put our stuff in the trash," she said, gathering their plates and cups. "You go investigate. I know you. You can't resist. Ha."

"I'm going to get closer," Cece said, ignoring Heidi's jab. She got up and moved to a closer table. She sat down a little over from and behind Dahlia's table where she could watch Dahlia and look around the yard with an unobscured view. She watched as Dahlia pulled out a cell phone enclosed in a shiny yellow case. She angled it high above her head so her selfie would feature an abundance of cleavage. Cece watched as she snapped a dozen shots, scrunching her eyebrows in concentration as she selected four or five. With a sniff of anticipation she punched send. She readjusted her short dress to expose another few inches of skin as she anxiously awaited "likes" like a hungry cat crouched under a bird feeder. The first ping broadened her smile to a gloat of satisfaction.

Heidi returned from the cleanup and sat down at the empty chair next to Cece.

"So how old do you think she is?" Cece asked.

"Not sure. She's at least in her fifties. She doesn't work for Santucci at all, probably hasn't for a pretty long time. I think he dumped her entirely after he got title to her house. My neighbor was at the Biltmore shopping center the other day and saw her. She's a sales lady in the men's department at Macy's."

"Ahh. That's funny. No surprise there. Probably trolling for a husband any way she can."

"You gotta hand it to her for chutzpa," Heidi sighed. "But to change the subject, I sort of envy you for getting Santucci's house. It's pretty over the top crazy garish. Everything's gold and marble. I just have the Encanto and Monte Vista Spanish boring mansion."

"Are you kidding? It's gorgeous. I love that house. But let's finish up. We've got a long day tomorrow. Have to be at our houses by nine, right?"

As Cece and Heidi trailed through the emptying tables heading for the street, Cece slipped off to the side and zigzagged around tables to pass the table where Dahlia lingered, absorbed in her phone. She sneaked a better look. Chutzpa indeed. Dahlia was definitely decked out in the same bright yellow sundress she had worn that morning despite the March evening chill, same dangly feathered earrings and bright yellow nail polish and enough makeup to make a Broadway actress look pale. She had a look, that was for sure.

"Come on," Cece nudged George the next morning. "Walk with me to Santucci's and then you can leave me there. We can take Nicky and you can get him back by yourself, right?"

"Sure," George nodded. "No problem. He doesn't want to skip his walk. He'd be depressed all day if that happened."

Cece smiled down at a furiously jumping and circling little dog who knew he was about to have a walk. "If you'd just be still for a moment I could make this happen a lot faster," she said, while holding Nicky's collar so she could slip the harness over his head.

Finally harnessed up and leash attached, Nicky, George and Cece headed up Thirteenth Avenue toward Santucci's house.

Nicky trotted ahead full of excitement for his adventure.

Orange blossoms in the air, the smell of spring in the desert city! What could be better? Sun rays sliced through the fronds of Palmcroft's hundred year old iconic palm trees that lined every street. Rye grass lawns glistened with the spray from early morning lawn sprinklers and the rosy-faced love birds were squawking in the canopies. Perfect morning, Cece smiled to herself. What a day for the tour.

As they rounded the curve heading onto Encanto Drive, Nicky froze. The scruffty orange cat that lived at a nearby homeless encampment slunk from under a India hawthorn hedge and raced toward the Santucci yard.

Nicky bolted, catching Cece off guard as the leash whipped from her grip. "Whoa," she gulped, startled by the unexpected yank. The cat flashed by and Nicky was off in hot pursuit, into the west end of Santucci's yard where the cat had slipped through a gate left ajar.

"Oh, no," she gasped. "Get him, George."

George harrumphed as his 68-year-old legs didn't exactly spring into action. Not one to wait, Cece dashed across the grass and through the gate in time to see the cat vanish over the back brick wall and Nicky at a dead stop with his leash snagged on a tree branch protruding at an odd angle from a large fish pond. As Cece ran to untangle the leash, her eyes raised to take in the pond itself. Gagging, she let out a terrified scream. Two bare legs with one flipflop dangling from a toe rose out of the water made murky by a rust red stain. Large koi nibbled at a pale ankle. Cece stared in horror before she pulled Nicky's leash free from the branch and fled, dragging poor Nicky behind.

"George, call 911. There's a body in the pond in there."

"What? Who? Is it Santucci?"

"I don't know," she panted, frantically. "It's two legs. That's all I can see. Here, take Nicky. Call the police and give them the address. I'll try the front door. Get someone to help."

Before George could rein in Nicky, Cece was at the door pushing the bell. No answer. She turned the knob but the door was closed tightly. She banged as hard as she could but nothing. "Let's go around back, let's pull him out, let's do something!!" She was beginning to sound overwrought, George thought.

"Slow down, Sherlock. I've called the police so let's just wait for them." But Cece was already through the gate, at the pond and pulling at a sickly grayish leg. George made it through in time to yell, "For heaven's sake, this could be a crime scene and you're interfering. That's a crime, you know!"

Cece gulped, "You're right. Sorry." She dropped the leg which splashed back into the murky water. "Whoever owns this leg is definitely a goner." She looked around, searching. "The side door's open. Maybe someone's there. Let's find help." With that Cece wheeled around and rushed across the side yard and up the steps, pushing the door farther open. She disappeared into the kitchen, leaving George shaking his head in disbelief.

"You're seriously demented," he muttered, squinting into the rays of the rising sun that now shown on an empty space in Cece's wake.

The kitchen was unlit and still dim in the early morning light. Cece couldn't help but gawk at the lavish monster range. A Cornue, of course. He probably can't even cook.

A sound, a creak of the floorboards, caught Cece mid-step. She froze, suddenly aware of her rather tenuous position. Heart pounding, she stared at the far door that was slowly opening.

CHAPTER THREE

A broom handle appeared first, followed by a uniformed body slowly backing into the room pulling a bucket along the tiled floor. As she turned, Cece gasped.

"Cuca!!! What on earth are you doing here?"

Startled at seeing her, Cuca's hand flew to her mouth, sending the broom clattering to the tiled floor. "Ms. Cece, what are YOU doing here?"

Cece rushed to Cuca's side, pushing her back through the partially opened door. "There's been an accident. I think it's Santucci outside, dead. I didn't even know you were working here. The police will be here in a minute so you better get ready. They'll ask some questions but if you need help, we'll help you."

Cuca had helped Cece with the housework while George was in the hospital after his heart attack. Cece had a motherly fondness for the young Oaxacan immigrant and had helped her with her immigration attorney. "For now, you better go back in the living room and wait."

Cece went back out the kitchen door and through the side gate to join George who was holding Nicky close to his side. They sat on the steps of the porch and waited. Soon a siren wailed close by and a police car rounded the corner and raced to the front of the house. The blue and white Phoenix PD van pulled to the curb and two cops jumped out.

"This way," Cece motioned them toward the open gate. In minutes the body was dragged from the pond. George and Cece crowded through the gate anxious to know who the victim was.

"Stand back," the uniformed cop commanded as Cece pushed against his back to get a better look. Santucci's water logged frame, looking limp and ghoulish in the morning light, was in stark contradiction to the beautiful spring morning.

Cece's legs wobbled to jelly and a roil of pain gripped her stomach. She gulped for air and, with a trembling voice, she whispered, "I didn't much like him but this is...is too awful. No one deserves this." She sighed and turned to George. His face had turned a few shades lighter and looked a bit queazy. With a start Cece jolted back. "The tour. I almost forgot. It starts in..." She glanced at her watch. "Twenty-five minutes. I'd better call Joyce. She'll need to know asap."

The crowds were already gathering at Encanto Park where tour tickets were selling at a hot pace. Vendors were setting up booths of food specialities, arts and crafts. Food wagons and musicians were getting ready. The place was humming with activity.

Cece raced through the growing crowd and met Joyce at the ticket booth. Joyce was the home tour coordinator. After explaining what happened, she queried Joyce. "What should we do? A lot of people already have their tickets and the Santucci house is definitely on the tour map."

"At least it's not one of the first houses to be reached so it'll be a while before people make it that far. For now we can cross out the house on all the tickets not yet sold. I'll get some volunteers on it."

"Sorry, Joyce. I need to get back to Santucci's. I left George being interviewed by the police and they want to talk to me too. I found the body. Well, Nicky did but he's not going to get the credit. I'll see you when we're done. Obviously the house is closed off so I'm not needed. Who on earth thought this could happen?"

"We should announce it over the loud speaker. Probably will sell even more tickets. A murder! *Quelle chance!* Everyone loves a murder!"

"Joyce, you're terrible."

"I'm kidding. I'm not going to say a murder much as I'd like to. I'll just say an unfortunate accident necessitates removing the house from the tour and leave it at that."

"Anyway we don't even know if it was a murder. Maybe he got drunk and drowned himself. Didn't exactly have a sterling reputation I gather."

"I guess we'll find out. But nobody liked him and his house was a garish disgrace to our refined and elegant neighborhood," Joyce sniffed with only a little hint of silly pretense. "If I remember right your George, *George the architect,*" she added emphasis, "said his house was an architectural abomination and he should be tarred and feathered and run out of town...or was it simply— shot."

"Goodness, don't remind me," Cece swallowed.

"He's probably already a suspect."

"Ha, ha. Bite your tongue, you terrible person."

"I'm sorry. Just kidding. I guess it's pretty macabre to be joking about it. The reality of death hasn't really sunk in. It's what happens when you read too many crime novels."

As Cece made it back to the Santucci house, the police were just finishing up with George. Yellow tape was strung around the yard, neighbors were gathering on the sidewalk and more police cars and an ambulance crowded the street. Paramedics were wheeling the cloth covered stretcher through the gate toward the ambulance. There was no hurry and the reality of death hit Cece harder than she realized.

George reached her side. "I think that was routine. They said they might want to talk to me again so not to leave town. Guess we'll have to reschedule our world tour."

"Very funny," Cece grumbled, no longer in the mood for lightness. "Me next."

The interview was short and to the point. After Cece explained again how and why they found the body, the police wrapped it up with the same admonition to not leave town. Cece was tempted to repeat the sarcastic world tour line but decided against it. She was suddenly anxious to get home and have a cup of coffee and something decadently sweet and soothing.

CHAPTER FOUR

The Monday evening the day after the tour, the Encanto-Palmcroft B and B book club decided they needed an emergency meeting. They had named themselves B and B book club for Books and Bonding. And bonding they did! The club meetings were a lively combination of book discussions, neighborhood gossip and life stories. For books they favored murder mysteries or psychological thrillers but they read anything that caught the fancy of any one of them. They had even done a few vintage Agatha Christie's. Although it was not the first Thursday of the month when they usually met, the events of the previous day caused such a stir, they decided they couldn't wait. A murder in the neighborhood! That was definitely an even better reason for a meeting than discussing their latest murder mystery book club choice.

"Emergency meeting tonight." Cece announced with barely constrained excitement.

"Book club, yet again? You ladies and Agatha Christie?" George queried with a ponderous sigh. "This means I'm going out for a beer with the guys."

"Good idea." Cece zoomed around the dining room snatching up the dinner plates, cups and other detritus from their meal and depositing it all into the kitchen sink. It was George's turn to clean up the kitchen so she was good to go. "Although we're not discussing Agatha obviously."

"So what are you discussing? The dead Santucci?" George's smile was turning south. Although he always supported Cece's endeavors, he was also not so blazé as to not think the ladies could be courting some real trouble. He already knew they thought they were personally responsible for the death since it happened in the neighborhood and on their home tour. And, he thought, they seemed just a little too excited to have a real death right under their noses.

"You know your Agatha Christie is about a century out of date. Don't think she would be solving any murders in today's world. I bet the police were more bumbling in Somerset or wherever it was that she lived. Our Phoenix boys are probably much more up to snuff."

"Sure," Cece sniffed. "Tell that to the good people of those lovely suburban towns of Gilbert and Queen Creek. Exactly how did the police solve their Preston Lord murder? Remember the kid murdered at the Halloween party?" she asked with more than a smack of sarcasm. "Oh, right. They didn't. If it hadn't been for the Arizona Republic reporters and neighborhood mothers, nothing would have happened. Those goons, the stupid teenage punks, would have gotten away with murder and general mayhem. So how did the police explain that? Not enough evidence, no new leads. Drop the case. Never mind the dozens of videos of the crimes. Teens film everything. All those beatings and it wasn't just the onlookers who filmed. The thugs themselves filmed their attacks and posted them on social media. Bragging!

And then they killed a kid, Preston Lord, that they had gang jumped and beaten while he lay helpless against them. So how were the police in the towns of Gilbert and Queen Creek so effective in making those towns safe….towns that were promoted as great places to raise a family? Ha! Good ole American suburbs. So was it gross incompetence or a coverup? Who knows."

"Okay, okay. You've got a point I have to admit," George conceded. "But the Santucci death is different. Anyway the police haven't released much information about it all. I would think they're still investigating."

"Maddie, from the book club, has an inside line and she says City Hall was buzzing all day. She's learned the latest news."

George turned in his chair to face Cece. That frown deepened, crinkling his forehead all along the worry lines already etched there.

"So you're sure it was a murder? Didn't you say Maddie found that out? How did she do that? I thought she was a court reporter. How does she have an inside line? It's not like she's a judge or a lawyer."

"She's clerking for the court. She's into everything and she's young and hot and all the judges, the men at least, are partial to her. That's how she has an inside line. You men, you're all so predictable."

Now it was George's turn to harrumph. He knew he'd lost that argument. He couldn't stop them or lessen their enthusiasm. Impossible!

Cece went to the hall closet to retrieve her jacket. Slipping it on, she waggled her fingers at George and disappeared into the hallway.

"Better take Nicky with you if you're walking over," George

called out from the other room. "He'll be your protector. I was kind of kidding, but seriously there actually could be a murderer around. You should drive just to play safe."

"I'm perfectly fine. Don't be such a worrywart. It's a beautiful evening with a gorgeous sunset to enjoy and I have my furry knight by my side. Anyway it's still light and only a few blocks away."

Before George had a chance to respond Cece had slipped out the door with Nicky right behind.

"Come on my ferocious little bodyguard," Cece said, while patting Nicky's head and slipping on his harness. "Let's go, Geronimo!" Nicky leapt up, pulling Cece across the patio, straining against the leash like he was an Iditarod sled dog.

They stepped into the darkening street heading north around the circle. Nicky was beyond excitement because the quarterly curbside pickup had started after being delayed in deference to the home tour. The city usually accommodated the Encanto-Palmcroft board requests for altering the pickup dates if there was a conflict with neighborhood social events. After all, the neighborhood had been home to so many Phoenix dignitaries over the years. No one wanted to see piles of broken furniture and other debris while wandering the streets during the home tour. So now there were endless piles to sniff out and who knows what could be found?

Maddie's house was a small cottage with a lovely bay window in front. It was one of the first built in Palmcroft by the founder of the Heard Museum, Dwight Heard, the son-in-law of the founder of what is now the True Value Hardware chain. He, like many others in the late nineteenth and early twentieth centuries, came to the desert southwest because of respiratory issues. It helped that he married the boss's daughter, Maie Bartlett, and then made his own fortune when the land that he purchased with his father-in-law along the Salt River exploded in value after the Roosevelt Dam was completed in 1911. A reliable water source transformed the desert into an oasis that Heard was quick to take advantage of. The fact that the water that now turned Encanto-Palmcroft into a lush suburb had previously nourished the crops of the Akimel O'odam people for hundreds of years was conveniently ignored. As Encanto-Palmcroft blossomed into a "high class development" according to the advertisements of the time, the Salt River downstream from Phoenix dried up leaving all the living things that relied on its waters to find another way to survive. Ah! progress.

However there was one bit of progress definitely linked to Maddie's house, Cece thought. Arizona's first woman governor, Rose Mofford, had once lived there. A very nice thought at that, Cece smiled to herself. Even though Rose wasn't actually elected. Which considering it was the 1980's wasn't so surprising. She got in by a fluke after Governor Ev Mecham, the Glendale car dealer, was impeached. She had been secretary of state, a basically glorified secretary's job, and Rose had been a secretary like so many smart women of her day. No one else much wanted the job, but a side benefit was a next in line to the governorship. How different today is, Cece thought. Now we have an elected woman governor and no matter who had won in the last election it would have been a woman!! Now that really is progress!

Cece stepped onto the low porch to the front door. Maddie, with her golden retriever Daisy at her side, answered the bell quickly and they led Cece and Nicky into the family room in the back of the house near the small but beautifully appointed kitchen. Nicky trotted along happily behind Daisy, their tails wagged joyfully as they headed for a corner where they could observe the people action.

Maddie was the youngest of the book club members. She was an imposing figure, tall and strong with long tawny hair that curled over her shoulders almost to her waist. Grey eyes and a big smile accompanied by an uninhibited and infectious laugh that gave her an aura of boundless energy. Now she was pulling out chairs for the group which, with Cece now there, numbered five.

"Sorry, ladies, so last minute but I really just got the word this afternoon. So get a glass and some snacks and I'll tell you what happened." After a flurry of drink pouring and plate filling, everyone settled back in their chairs and turned waiting eyes on Maddie. "The police have brought in Dahlia for questioning," she continued to some small gasps in the room. "Someone had heard her threatening Santucci a few days ago. Very public. She was screaming at him, threatening to make things right with her mother's house. Said she had a paper trail. Some kind of contract that she claimed Santucci signed. He laughed in her face, called her an old whore and said he'd never had anything to do with her. He didn't like old women with sagging cheeks and boobs. He actually poked her cheek and sneered. Dahlia went ballistic, threatening to kill him. So anyway apparently the police now consider her a suspect."

That caused a stir. "I think I might have done the same," Anne grumbled. Anne was a social worker with a long career helping troubled people so the group often turned to her for an opinion.

"What do you think?" Heidi asked Anne. "Could Dahlia be a murderer?"

"She seems pretty troubled to me," Anne volunteered. "But have they definitely ruled out an accident? Do they have an autopsy yet?"

"I don't think so. It takes awhile," Maddie answered. "But there's talk that he was pretty drunk. His blood alcohol level was high. Apparently he had a swim party in his heated pool that night. Some of the strippers from his Scottsdale club were there. They were pretty raucous for a bunch of "ladies." Maddie air quoted. "But how drunk do you have to be to fall into your fish pond and hit your head against the side hard enough to drown?"

"Good question. But Dahlia? I think she could have done it. She's a gym rat. I see her all the time at LA Fitness pumping iron. Pretty damn fit," Heidi said.

Cece suppressed a snicker. "I can just picture her with bar bells. But seriously she's probably strong but he's a beast. Short and heavy and maybe drunk. No spring chicken himself, so who knows. I think it's possible. She could have done it. I saw the look on her face when he yelled at her the day before the tour. Sheer hatred. It was striking."

"And another thing I learned," Maddie continued. "Did you guys know he had an ocelot in a cage in his backyard?"

"Wha-a-at!" they all chorused. Maddie got up to open another bottle of *pinot noir.*

"That's crazy," Stephanie chimed in, raising her glass for a refill. "That calls for another glass. But aren't they endangered? You can't have an ocelot in captivity. They're wild."

"Well, apparently you can. You have to have a license but if you do, it's legal."

"Why would Santucci want a wild animal? He doesn't have that big a yard. It's not like his ugly house is some kind of Neverland. He just seems weirder and weirder," Cece said.

Stephanie chewed on her lip. Her long hair and bangs framed a thoughtful looking face that radiated a mid-western plain talk sensibility. She was a school counselor at West High and like Anne, always interested in analyzing the neighborhood eccentrics. Her background in psychology and counseling gave her a perspective that the group all appreciated. "Men could think owning wild animals makes them look macho. Dominance over the wild beasts. Isn't that what it's all about? Big game hunters…"

"Like that Florida doctor who shot lions illegally. Ha, ha. Wannabe tough guys!" Heidi added.

"The really worst part is, the ocelot is missing."

That got everyone's attention. "There's a cage in the back of the house and the door was open when the police got there yesterday morning. The ocelot was gone." With that bit of news Maddie lifted the bottle, frowned at it and went back into the kitchen for another.

"Holy crap, is it in the neighborhood? Has anyone spotted it? There're so many bushes and overgrown areas. The park!!" Anne exclaimed with a look of complete horror. Anne, like Cece, was a gardener and knew every exotic plant in the neighborhood. She also volunteered in the public rose garden, pruning and deadheading all spring. She was well aware of the abundant vegetation in the neighborhood.

"I think there's going to be a neighborhood alert tonight. Ocelots are nocturnal so it's not surprising that it hasn't been seen yet." Maddie refilled some glasses and sat back with a plop. She twisted her long hair anxiously, looking down at her sleeping golden retriever and said, "I think we all have pets. So be really careful with them. Ocelots are pretty small, but bigger than a house cat, dangerous and wild. It's probably hungry and it could kill a little dog…. like Nicky."

CHAPTER FIVE

All eyes turned to Nicky who had been edging closer to Daisy, hoping to get the now sleeping dog to respond to him. Hearing his name, he froze, looking up at all his human friends and wagged his tail hopefully. Was everything all right? The ladies who were always so joyful now looked decidedly unhappy. That was bad news. He would have to do some doggy thinking. That was the answer. Nicky hid his head under his paws. Something was definitely up. He would find out, he decided. But for now he turned his attention back to Daisy.

"Speaking of wild animals, you know there are other people who have a pretty passionate dislike of Sal Santucci. You all know that guy, the retired wildlife biologist. His yard is a certified wildlife habitat. It was on the home tour last time. The swimming pool is now a huge koi pond and mallards nest there too. It's an amazing place. There was a neighborhood board meeting two months ago and Santucci was there trying to drum up support for a new club he wants to build on the land from the northeast corner of Fifteenth Avenue and McDowell all the way north past the garden club and the rose garden. All the way to the tennis courts. Needless to say the reception to that idea was ice cold. You all know Brett. As the board president he's good at putting people in their place. Whether they want it or not. But Santucci needed it. He swore at Brett right in front of everyone. Created quite a scene."

"Wait, that's crazy," Anne interrupted. "The vacant lot is one thing but the garden club and rose garden are public. He can't tear them down to build whatever he wants."

"Unfortunately, he can," Heidi interjected. Heidi, the fit and forthright— Cece always thought about her that way. A waist the size of my thigh, she sighed shifting her weight to look a little thinner.

"I'm on the board, remember, so obviously I was at that meeting," Heidi continued. "He can't do anything now because that land and the buildings on it are part of a hundred year lease but that lease will soon be up. Everyone just takes it for granted that the club and gardens will always be there for everyone to enjoy but that's not the case. Once the lease is up, the land could be developed any way the city wants."

"But surely no one would want to destroy something as iconic to the neighborhood and the city as the garden club and the rose garden."

"Think tax money coming in. Big resorts bring in big bucks. That's all a lot of those politicians care about."

"The point is," Anne continued. "Fred Spencer, he's the biologist—he was there and he attacked not only Santucci's plan but after the meeting adjourned he got into a heated argument with Santucci in the parking lot about the ocelot. Fred knew Santucci had it and threatened to have it removed for improper care and habitat. So," she added, "between the dust up with Brett and then Spencer, the tension at the board meeting was off the charts.

Santucci yelled that Fred was a nobody and had no authority to do anything. Which of course was pretty much true since Fred has been retired for awhile and never was very high ranking in the bureaucracy. He is a little odd, I must say. Nice, but a bit untamed himself, at least socially."

"Yeah, I remember meeting him at one of the schmoozes last fall," Stephanie mused, thinking about the neighborhood gatherings. Sunday afternoon schmoozes are held on someone's front patio every month. People volunteer their front patios, driveways or yards for a BYOB social gathering. At least 50 people typically show up for an afternoon of socializing and getting to know their neighbors. "He was decidedly odd. He was wearing basically rags for clothes. You didn't see it at first but once you got close to him you could see how threadbare his shirt was. His shoes were held together with the shoelaces. He's a bachelor but still. No matter if he's not rich he could get a decent outfit for a few bucks at Goodwill. He did seem friendly and… well, like you said, Anne, odd. Not creepy odd, just odd. Dahlia was there as usual. Sniffing around for a paramour I suppose. And she didn't even bother to chat him up for more that a few minutes. Didn't sniff the sweet smell of greenbacks I guess."

"So we all agree," Cece interjected. "Lots of people didn't like Santucci. George even had some pretty unpleasant words about him that he hasn't exactly hidden. Sal and his abomination of a house. And George wouldn't hurt a fly. So just because all these people have been in rows with him doesn't mean they'd murder him."

Maddie held up a bottle of red. "Anyone?" She peered around the group all of whom were suddenly thoughtful. No one moved. "OK," She put down the bottle and grabbed a handful of popcorn. "So it's my job to get the lowdown at the courthouse. I'll see if anyone else has been brought in for questioning and let you guys know. In the meantime try to remember what you can. Anything that might be a lead."

"And what exactly are we supposed to do with our 'leads?'" Heidi asked. "We could get a meeting with the detectives who are investigating the case. You know how on tv they always hand out their cards and say, "Contact me any time if you can think of anything.""

"Not sure that's how it works in real life," Cece said. "We're a bunch of old ladies…forgive me Maddie, not you, but us others. Or some more than others," she back peddled. "Or me at least. Do you think they'll pay any attention to us? Not so sure."

"So we just scout around on our own and see what turns up, right?" Cece looked quizzically at the others. They all nodded. "There're other ways to get information than police interviews." With that Cece called to Nicky, pulling his leash out of her bag and got up to leave. "We got work to do!!"

The walk home was as short as the walk over but somehow it seemed interminable. Darkness seeped around the corners of houses that seemed less friendly than they had been just a few hours ago. Moonlight cast long-armed shadows from the palm trees, crisscrossing the sidewalk with strange shapes. The fronds turned to ragged claws scraping across the curbs. Cece shivered, her light weight jacket feeling as threadbare as Fred's shirt. She pulled it closer around her neck as Nicky again stopped to sniff a pile of construction debris at the edge of the street. Would an ocelot hide in a construction pile? Or a murderer? The thought flitted uncomfortably through Cece's mind. She couldn't help but think of the beautiful homes on yesterday's tour and how the night darkness revealed another way to see the neighborhood. Light and darkness. How transformative they seemed. Which was real? One? Both? She pulled Nicky away from the pile of trash. Reluctantly he trotted on a few steps and then stiffened, his little body shaking with alarm.

Jolted out of her musing, Cece looked at Nicky and whispered in a quavering voice, "What is it? What do you see?"

A breeze picked up, scuttling the clouds over the half moon. Darkness settled deeper into the trees and the street blurred as if a fog had descended, obscuring the outlines of familiar things. Why hadn't the city replaced the burned out bulbs in the streetlights by her house? Everyone loved the art nouveau street lamps so different from those in the rest of Phoenix with their high glaring lights. The mellow glow from the vintage lamp posts enhanced the quaint charm of the neighborhood, but now Cece would have been happy for any light to cast away the gloom that enveloped the street.

She looked down at Nicky's shaking body and followed his gaze just in time to see a fleeting shadow slipping behind an oleander hedge and vanish into the darkened side yard of her neighbor's house. A cat? No, too big, too vertical. Gone too fast to see anything for sure. Cece yanked at Nicky's leash and fled for her front door.

CHAPTER SIX

The morning sun shone through the Venetian blinds just enough to waken Cece from a fitful night's sleep. She stretched, yawned and snapped out of her sleepy fog with a jolt of memory from the night before. The shadow! She rolled over, glancing at George's still sleeping lump under the covers. Better not to mention that encounter to him, worrier that he was. Nicky shuffled out of his doggy slumber in the center of the king size bed to rub his nose against Cece's shoulder.

"Good morning, sweet pea," she whispered as she ruffled his salt and pepper shaggy fur. "I hope you slept better than I did." She slipped out of bed and tiptoed across the room into the hall. A little coffee to get the juices flowing, she thought.

After the usual breakfast of Cheerios and blueberries, Cece poured a final cup of coffee. George was lingering over the morning paper. They had already discussed at length the long article with photographs about Sal Santucci and his suspicious death. Still under investigation. Police were following leads.

"Look," he held up the paper, pointing at a column toward the bottom of the page. "There's an article about the ocelot that escaped. That didn't take long. It's funny but the article also mentioned the sighting of a wild ocelot less than a year ago."

"Yeah, I read that," Cece added. "In the Huachuca Mountains. That's a long way from here. It's the northern extent of their range from the Mexican Sierra Madres. But I remember that it said male ocelots could travel hundreds of miles to find a mate. Poor guy, that's what he probably had to do since his sighting in Arizona was the first in over fifty years!"

Nicky had claimed his spot under the dining room table and was half listening to his two-leggeds' talk. He picked up the sense that they were talking about that thing, what was it? The one that ate little dogs! He would have to be even more on guard than usual.

"I'm going strong on my drawings," George said, finishing off his toast and folding the newspaper. Laying it on the table, he rose and stretched. "I'm hoping to have the plans completed by the beginning of the summer."

George and Cece had bought a small wooded lot in Prescott at almost 6000 feet elevation. After George's heart attack he had been pretty much ordered to stop working and concentrate on taking it easy. So he had turned his attention to what had been a long time dream of his, a mid-century modern "cabin" in a place with cool summers. The lot in Prescott filled the bill. Unfortunately it also was filled with boulders and a difficult access road and other problems. Enough to keep him busy at his drafting board and out of trouble, Cece thought. It also kept him busy enough that he barely noticed her constant goings in and out. Just as well!

Just then Cece heard loud crunching noises coming from the street. Nicky jumped up on his ottoman perch by the dining room window that overlooked the front of the house and the street. Ears perked, he barked a protest at a backhoe rumbling into a pile of oleander branches across the street in front of the Parker house. So cleanup time. The quarterly curbside pickup had started.

Cece watched from the dining room table as she sipped her coffee. The debris around the neighborhood had become a source of controversy because whenever trash was left out for any length of time it was an open invitation to the residents of the homeless encampment on the vacant lot at Fifteen and Mc-Dowell to scarf up prizes to take back to add to the piles of trash already there.

Ever since the city had cleared out the huge downtown encampment called the Zone, a scattering of those displaced moved into the vacant lot to take advantage of its proximity to downtown and the shade trees and water available at Encanto Park. The homeless shuffle. Just move things around and pretend the problem has been dealt with.

Thinking of the encampment just a few blocks away, the shadowy figure from last night flicked through her mind. After she downed the last of her coffee, she pulled out her cell phone and dialed the one person she most wanted to spent time with this morning. Anne.

When Cece arrived at Anne's front porch, she hesitated, listening to the chords of a piano from inside. Anne was an accomplished pianist and often played in her church and at some of the school functions. With her cool Nordic looks, blonde hair cut in a wedge and classic features, she was beautiful to behold,

Cece thought. She was snapped back to the present by the click of the handle, as Anne opened the door, hands on hips, and demanded in only a slightly sarcastic voice, "And what are you up to now? I'm suspicious. But come on in." Cece pulled Nicky along behind her into Anne's house. Somewhat breathlessly, she described the encounter at the trash pile from the night before.

"The more I've thought about it, which was often all night," Cece continued with a frown, "the more I think it might have been that woman from the homeless camp. The one they call Crazy Carrie."

"It's unsheltered, not homeless," Anne admonished. "Or unhoused if you prefer. Or people experiencing home…."

"Okay, okay, miss pc police. You know what I mean and anyway I'm not so sure what the difference is between homeless and unhoused. Aren't they the same thing?"

"You know Andy. He follows the city's guidelines and that includes saying "unhoused" regardless of semantics." Anne sighed but was smiling as well.   Anne's husband worked for Phoenix's Office of Housing Solutions, a newly established branch of the Department of Economic Security set up to tackle the growing problem of a burgeoning population of drifters, addicts and the mentally ill perpetually stressed for places to stay and ways to survive.

A huge number of homeless had lived downtown over several blocks of solid squalor dubbed the Zone. Tents, tarps, junk everywhere. Drugs, fights, illegal trashcan fires, even a murder. The nearby business owners sued the city for letting it go unchecked and they won in court. So the city was forced to take action and the cleanup began. It took a number of weeks for everyone and their belongings to be moved out but the new problem was where do they go? Once the Zone was cleaned up, the residents were supposedly placed in other shelters but everyone knew there were not enough places and that many did not want to live in shelters under the city's rules and regulations. So small encampments started popping up all around the inner city and even beyond, north of the I-10. Bus shelters were commandeered, parks provided shelter and there were even hapless bodies just lying on the sidewalk until prodded to move on. A seemingly insolvable situation.

"I want to find Carrie and try to see if she knows anything. I think she was the one I saw last night. The figure was small, surely a woman. Maybe she has seen things, knows things that we don't. It's worth a try. And I've brought water bottles for an offering!"

"*Quid pro quo*," Anne said. "Water for intel."

"Something like that."

Anne hesitated. "You know there're some pretty rough people in those camps. Do you really think it's safe?" She twisted her hands and grimaced, anxiety flicking across her face. "I hear a lot of unsavory stuff from Andy. I know they don't usually bother people outside their encampment but no guarantees."

"It's broad daylight. I've got my cell phone. Got my guard dog and can run for cover if needed. I'm going. You don't have to come." Cece turned her face down, coughing softy into her hand with a "scaredy cat" barely audible.

"Oh, okay. I'm not going to miss out on this little adventure. Let me get some tennies on and I'll be ready. But don't you ever breathe a word of this to Andy. He'd have a fit!"

Soon the two women, with Nicky in tow, headed south and west, passing the lovely Tudor cottages, Spanish revivals and

Craftsmen bungalows and onto the bleak emptiness of the vacant lot at the end of west McDowell Road. It didn't take long to find the newly set up squatters' tarps stretched over woompy-jawed grocery carts and broken lawn furniture. Like the nomadic Apaches that had crossed over the land centuries earlier, their encampments were quickly constructed and just as quickly deconstructed, as necessary. Wasn't that the history of humanity, Cece mused, scanning the mostly empty lot just south of the public spaces of the Phoenix garden club and rose garden. Always the newcomers pushing out those who stood in their way and then not wanting them hanging around close by to remind the newcomers of their infringement. Or the settled people nervous about the nomadic people in their midst—the gypsies, the traveling salesman, the sailors—seeing them as possible threats. But of course this was a different problem but still, it was one group with power ousting another group without power.

As Cece and Anne approached a small grove of trees providing a minimum of shade and privacy, Nicky slowed and started to tremble ever so slightly. His ears perked up and a low growl rumbled from his throat. He smelled cats, and other things, strange other things! He was acutely aware that this was not a usual kind of place. One thing for sure, he thought. Cats. Wild cats. They smelled differently from house cats. They smelled of rats and birds, not cat chow. This was a place of things he did not know.

"How will you know which tent she's in?" Anne looked in dismay at the tumultuous heaps of trash, shopping carts, tarps and cardboard boxes.

"Actually I saw her, I think, the other day. She was wheeling a grocery cart into that area. I was curious and watched her while

I was stopped at the light. I'm pretty sure she's in that one." Cece nodded toward a brown tarp lying haphazardly across two shopping carts, with enough junk piled around the edges to obscure any way to see inside.

They moved slowly in that direction as Nicky continued his low rumble. "Shush, Nicky." Cece pulled at his leash. "You're the intruder here. Mind your manners," she said barely louder than a whisper. She knew that Nicky like all dogs could smell odors unavailable to humans. Fear, anxiety, hunger. So much more than orange blossoms and dinner cooking. What did he smell? she wondered. What state of being could he detect not privy to humans? The three of them, the ladies and dog, hesitated a moment as they neared the makeshift tents.

At that moment a scruffy yellow cat darted out one of the nearest tarp's open flap.

Nicky jumped strongly, yanking Cece so hard that she almost toppled over. She bent and grabbed his collar and quickly dug into her pocket for the air spray can that could make Nicky freeze mid lunge. The yellow cat disappeared behind the trash piled up along side the tarp.

A small and wizened face jutted out from the tarp opening. A woman of indeterminate age pushed herself halfway through the opening in the makeshift tent shoving aside an overstuffed backpack that had blocked the entrance. She was wrapped in a blanket so old and filthy that its color or pattern was no longer distinguishable. Her dark red hair was coiled on top of her head in what could kindly be called a messy bun. Inserted into the top of it was a limp and faded artificial flower. A peony perhaps in its better days. Dark sunglasses were thrust against her forehead neither on her eyes nor on top of her head, giving her the visage of an alien bug. A bony cat claw finger pulled out from the folds of the blanket.

She stared at Cece and Anne, eyes darting back and forth between them, wordless and hostile. Then her beady eyes shifted to Nicky who seemed to be trying to scrunch himself up into becoming smaller. She wore a long sleeved black teeshirt with a shiny rhinestone bracelet encircling her wrist. She pointed at Nicky who slunk into the dirt trying to squeeze himself behind Cece.

"We, er, we thought you might like some water," Anne ventured, holding out a bottle with a shaking hand. The face eyed them suspiciously and looked back down at Nicky crouched a few feet away.

"Dogs, dogs, devils." She drew out her words slowly and pointed her finger closer to Nicky who was uncharacteristically subdued, peering out from behind Cece but at full alert. "Take it away. It steals, … it takes, it eats," and her skinny arm poked out from the blanket and waved around her as if there were hordes of dogs like hyenas waiting in the wings, gobbling up her things. She sank down on the ground and slumped forward as if suddenly asleep.

Cece and Anne glanced quickly at each other and then both sat on the ground too. Cece placed a water bottle down in front of Carrie. Of course Carrie wasn't really her name. A newspaper reporter writing about the Zone had named a woman there Carrie because she had allegedly burned down her tent with her boyfriend inside. Images of Steven King obviously inspired the name. Whether she murdered him or not had never been determined. And no one knew where she had gone after the Zone was abandoned. At least Anne and Cece didn't know but somehow the name seemed to fit.

"I'm Cece and this is Anne," Cece began and tried to keep her voice from trailing off as Carrie's eyes seem to roll back in her head. "We want to help," she continued shifting her weight to try for a more comfortable position. "We want you and the others to know there's a wild cat, an ocelot, that's escaped from a cage in the neighborhood. It might be a danger to you…and your cats," she added noticing a whiskered nose protruding from the tarp. "It hasn't been fed so it has to be hungry. Maybe you've seen it?" She paused hopefully, waiting for a response.

Carrie's eyes opened suddenly and blinked. Her body snapped back up with an agility that seemed to not belong to her wizened face. "No, no-o-o-o, cats are not danger. My cats, they don't eat your dogs," Carrie growled. "My cats, my cats, they like rats. It's the others that are a danger." Her tongue flicked out like a rattlesnake's and slid around her cracked lips. "Yes, rats and mice, little dishes of delight." She cackled softly, rubbing her blanket as if to dry her hands after a messy meal of rats and mice. Her head slumped down to her chest again.

"But we're talking about a wild cat, not your cats. It's an ocelot. Bigger than a cat with spots like a jaguar. It's dangerous to your cats as well as the dogs." Anne was getting a little exasperated. "We want you to be careful. You and the others here. Have you seen anything?" She tried again.

"I see, I see….everything. Yes, everything. I see the night things, those things, I know them. Yes, I do."

"What night things? Who do you know?" Cece tried to quell the tremor in her voice as she edged a little closer until only a few inches was keeping them apart.

"I see them. The others, they go where they shouldn't be. I

know, I know….everything. It will be bad, oh very bad. Yes, I know that. Ahh yes, tomorrow. Soon."

"But what? What will be bad?" Cece insisted, a spike of nerves crawling up her throat.

At that moment a small grey cat pushed out of a carton in the junk pile and, spotting Nicky, let out a ferocious hiss, arching its back ready for battle. Nicky, forgetting everything else, tried to bolt forward but Cece had a tight hold of his collar.

Carrie's eyes shot open. "Leave. Take your devil dog with you. Out, out, ouuuut," she hissed softly in a voice made scarier by its very softness. She retreated into the tarp and yanked down the flap that hit the ground with a thud, stirring up a small cloud of dust that quickly dissipated into the cool spring air.

"That went well." Anne said with a frown after they had gathered themselves up and turned to leave.

"I shouldn't have brought Nicky." Cece sighed as they walked back to the sidewalk. "Anyway I'm not so sure it was a total loss. What about all the business about her knowing who's out there. Maybe she does know something. Maybe she was scarfing around, looking for stuff, the night Santucci was killed."

"That's a lot of maybes. Not sure what we can do with all that. I don't think we can get anything coherent out of her." Anne looked dejected.

They walked on, passing the garden club and turning east on Palm Lane. "Everything is so pretty here. Maybe too pretty." The thought of Carrie sneaking around in the dark was creepy. "Do you think there's something more about her than just "off the rails"? It's like she sees things that maybe we can't see."

"What do you mean? Like she's a witch!"

"Of course not. I didn't mean that. It's just that we're not nosing around in the middle of the night. We just assume everyone is like us, in bed asleep. But…" Anne hesitated, chewing on her lower lip. "It's just that she seemed kind of tapped into a part of this neighborhood that we can't see. Things we don't know. Do you think she's warning us?"

"Like, beware the ides of March?" Cece said and then stopped dead and stared at Anne, eyes wide. "Good lord, the tour was the day after the ides of March! If Santucci was killed before midnight he was murdered on the ides of March."

"What on earth are you talking about?"

"Beware the ides of March. Shakespeare's play. Didn't you have to read *Julius Caesar* in high school English?

"Oh who knows. That was way too long ago. But…. yes, I think we did. Yeah, the soothsayer. He warned Caesar about the next day. And the rest is history."

"So what do you think? Carrie's a soothsayer? A fortune teller? What did she mean about tomorrow? Like something bad is going to happen." Cece laughed nervously. "This is ridiculous. She's just a poor, ill cat lady. Not a miserable one but a sort of powerful one, if anything. I don't think too many people would mess with her. Which is good, don't you think?"

"No, it's not good. Nothing about that life is good. Don't romanticize it, believe me. I know way too much, thanks to Andy's work. It's really pretty depressing." Anne sighed and shook her head slowly.

"Oh cheer up." Cece glanced down at Nicky who was now happily sniffing every bush they passed. He seemed to have forgotten the scary encounter and moved on to life as usual. "She has her cats and she is interesting if nothing else. Our Politicians should visit her. See what's going on."

"Ha, ha. She'd probably scare the pants off any politician that came snooping around!"

CHAPTER SEVEN

Stacey Hatcher was the only book club member with a pre-teen child. Her daughter Ollie B was ten and considered herself the president of the kids' club. Stacey, and two other neighborhood moms, ran the program that arranged activities for the neighborhood kids. Unfortunately the children in the neighborhood tended to go to different schools so it wasn't like the old days when all the kids went to Kenilworth Elementary and they could always find someone to hang out with any time, after school, in the summer or on weekends. Now there were public schools, private schools, charter schools, alternative schools, home schooling, you name it. So the kids' club played an important role in bonding the neighborhood, kids and moms.

There was a movement afoot it seemed, an attempt to promote a more laid back, less programed life for the children. But Stacey knew it was an uphill battle to convince parents that their kids didn't have to have endless scheduled activities to fill up every second of their time in the hopes it would keep them safe and off social media.

The kids' club had run a lemonade and baked goods stand during the home tour and pulled in over two thousand dollars.

And now the money had been tabulated, the check written and it was time to present it to the kids' club charity of choice, Liberty Wildlife Center. Stacey had alerted the center about the upcoming donation and they had been invited to come over for a small presentation as well as a personal tour of the facilities.

Stacey called Cece to see if she wanted to go to the center with them and of course she did. Stacey was a younger member of the book club. Her long dark luxurious hair swept back around her ears and curled around her shoulders. Her face had the glow of youth despite being in her forties and she managed to look serene no matter what craziness Ollie B and her friends were up to. She might not always be serene, Cece thought, but she always looked serene. Half the battle!

To Cece's way of thinking she was an ideal influence on the neighborhood kids, encouraging them to appreciate the natural world and also guiding them in developing a sense of responsibility for that world. She was a natural educator, and her influence already showed in Ollie B's developing personality. Cece had to smile just looking at Stacey and Ollie B together. Ollie B had all of her mother's qualities for energy and enthusiasm for the world around them.

Stacey came out of her house with Ollie B right behind her. She was carrying a large cardboard facsimile of a check. "Look at what we made," Ollie B exclaimed, holding it up for Cece to see. "It was my idea. Kind of like those sweepstakes checks. Pretty cool, huh?"

"I think it's a great idea to show off the donation. The idea that you kids worked so hard on the stand and made so much money is just amazing. I think you deserve all the attention you can get."

"Plus, they're giving it to such a good cause. They really care about the world and all the creatures in it." Stacey hugged Ollie B and gave her shoulders a little shake. "Ollie B's friend found a pigeon that had been wounded by a feral cat and they took it to the center. The center cared for it and nursed it back to health!"

"Yay, flying rats!" Cece muttered.

"But they don't judge. Pigeons are birds like any other bird. It needed help and that was all that mattered."

"Yes, yes. I agree," Cece mumbled, chastised. "All God's creatures is really true. Not for us humans to pick and choose according to our tastes."

With that decided, they crowded into Stacey's SUV's front seat, squeezing Ollie B between them. The check was stowed in the back seat. They headed east on McDowell to 24th Street where they turned south. As they passed to the west of the airport runways, a purple and orange Southwest plane dropped out of the sky so close it seemed to skim the top of their car.

"Wow," said Ollie B. "That was close. I think I ducked."

They laughed.

Passing through the airport, they crossed the mostly dry bed of the Salt River and turned off on the first street south of the river that led into the parking lot in front of the center.

"I hope Fred is volunteering today," Stacey said. "Maybe he knows something about the ocelot." She pulled into an empty parking space.

They gathered up their things and Ollie B pulled the huge check from the back seat. Once everyone was out, they headed down a sidewalk and through the double glass doors that led into the reception area and gift shop of the center. Once they were seated in the reception area and had explained their mission, a volunteer disappeared through a pair of doors to fetch the director, Gary Nugent. In a few minutes he appeared and headed to their group. He welcomed them to the center and waited while Ollie B hoisted up the large cardboard check and announced that it was a gift from the kids' club of Encanto-Palmcroft. After profuse thanks and a number of photographs both for the center to display and for publication in the neighborhood monthly magazine, Ollie B, Stacey and Cece followed a volunteer docent through the doors to a large shaded patio area. A koi and lily pond was centered in front of a long string of buildings that housed the rehabilitation rooms for treating the sick and injured birds and animals that were brought to the center. Although their focus was on birds, particularly predator birds, owls and raptors, they also had an array of snakes, lizards and geckos and small desert mammals.

As the volunteer explained the activities of each area, Cece, Stacey and Ollie B wandered along the windowed fronts of the examination and interactive rooms, watching with fascination. At the end of the buildings just before the raptor cages, a small group of visitors had seated themselves on a horseshoe shaped cement bench. An older man stood before them with a large Harris hawk resting on a leather cuff encircling his outstretched arm. He was obviously telling the group something that held their rapt attention. Cece, Stacey and Ollie B slipped in at the back and quietly listened to his lecture. Another volunteer soon joined the first. He had a peregrine falcon on a similar cuff on his arm. The two then explained the differences between falcons and hawks—how they hunted and how they survived even in the fifth largest city in the nation.

After the talk finished, the group filed off to see the captive birds too wounded to be released into the wild. Cece and Stacey looked around to see if Fred was there. They had discussed in advance the matter of the ocelot and Fred. "He might not want to talk about it since he was known to be very angry at Santucci over it. And now it's gone and Santucci's dead. Not a rosy picture for Fred, I'm afraid," Cece said.

The three headed down a dusty trail toward the river bed. The damming upstream on the Salt River left little water below the artificially constructed Tempe Town Lake. Here, west of the artificial lake, the river bed was no more than muddy puddles and desert scrub. But it was a beautiful afternoon with sunshine and cool breezes, a perfect day to explore the habitat. Up ahead they saw another small group of people listening to what was obviously a talk being given by one of the docents. It was Fred Spencer.

"Let's join the group," Cece whispered, as they neared the dozen or so listeners.

Fred was speaking softly but the quietness of the setting allowed his voice to carry. The hum of distant planes descending into Sky Harbor was not enough to cover his soft words. Cece watched him intently. He was maybe late fifties, a rather nice looking man but one who seemed to carry a weight on his shoulders, a certain sadness infused his voice and slumped his wiry frame. Maybe it was because of the injured animals that inhabited the center, their rehabilitation the focus of the organization. Was he drawn to help injured animals to cover the injuries in his own life? Cece mused.

She had heard that some time ago he had left the wildlife biology doctoral program at ASU. Some problem had developed but no one seemed to know exactly what it was. He had worked for the Fish and Game department for many years but was now in early retirement as far as she knew. The neighborhood knew him mainly because of his yard that was entirely devoted to being a certified wildlife habitat. He had inherited the home from his parents and Fred had spent most of his life there. He seemed to exist within that yard much as the animals did, quiet and unseen. He lived alone, whether out of choice or necessity, Cece didn't know. His swimming pool was long ago transformed into a duck pond and many rare and unusual plants cascaded over every cranny of his property. It was really a wonder for a suburban yard such as his to exist within the virtual center of a huge bustling city. When you looked closely though, weren't there oddities everywhere, hidden in almost every neighborhood? Cece thought.

As Fred finished up his talk and the people around him drifted away, he turned to Cece, Stacey and Ollie B. He approached them, smiling awkwardly. "Don't I know you ladies? You're from the neighborhood."

"Hi Fred," Stacey began. "Right, we are." She introduced her daughter Ollie B explaining about the kids' club donation to the center. "Ollie B just presented the kids' club check to Mr. Nugent but we thought that since we're here we would say hello."

Fred smiled and nodded without comment.

"We were wondering about the ocelot," she continued. "Have you heard anything? Has it been spotted?"

Fred shook his head sadly. "No, so far no one has seen it. Not been spotted. But it is spotted!" He paused noticing their look of confusion. "Sorry, that's just a little joke," he said awkwardly.

"Oh, right!. It's spotted, of course. Ha, ha!"

"Stupid of me," Fred mumbled. He continued, "We're hoping

it is either found quickly or it escapes into the river bed where it can travel great distances without much interference."

"Do you think we'll ever know?" Cece asked.

"Hard to say. If it's a male, it could travel many, many miles in a fairly short time and with luck be out of harm's way. We contacted the police after they searched the house but they said they couldn't find any records for the cat at the Santucci house and of course the owner is now dead. Unfortunately if it's a female, she could stay hidden nearby. She could stake out a territory where she is familiar with the food sources. A lot of people are leaving out cat food for our many neighborhood feral cats. Plus the park has mice, rabbits and this is the time for babies. A pretty good food supply for a natural cunning predator."

Cece gulped, thinking of her bird feeders with a constant bevy of sparrows, doves and occasionally love birds and grosbeaks. Before, she was only worried about feral cats but an ocelot would be on a whole different level. Not to mention Nicky who with terrier bravado would probably taunt a mountain lion not to mention an ocelot.

Fred continued, "Our contact with the police was kind enough to listen to me. He said they don't know anything about the cat and all records seem to be lost or who knows. I don't think they're prioritizing the cat. They don't know if it had any connection to Santucci's death but they're acting like they don't think so. Knowing a little about the kind of guy Santucci was I think the cat could have been black market, in which case it would be nearly impossible to trace. If it stays in the area, sooner or later it's going to cause problems. My real fear is that if someone manages to catch it, it could be killed for its pelt or sold illegally in the exotic animal trade circles. Either way, it's not good news for an ocelot." He shifted from foot to foot, gazing above their shoulders as he spoke.

Fred glanced over to the path leading down from the center and saw a new group gathering. "Sorry ladies, I have another lecture to give, so I need to be going."

"Sure, Fred. So good to see you. We love the work you're doing."

"Bye," they chorused.

"What do you think?" Cece posed the question with a frown, her eyes following Fred as he hobbled down the trail toward the waiting group. "He was unusually chatty. Does he seem like he could have been involved? Like he snuck over there and released the ocelot?"

"I don't know. But did you notice how he hardly looked at us directly. He was always looking above us like a flock of birds might fly by any time."

"Maybe that's just shyness. You know, like you can't look someone in the eye. Social awkwardness."

"That could be," Stacey conceded.

"What if he did do it? We don't even know when the cat escaped. And anyway how would Fred get into his backyard where the cage was? And how did he even know it was there? Nobody else seemed to know about it. But Fred confronted Santucci about it at the board meeting a month or so ago. So obviously he knew Santucci had the ocelot."

Stacey broke in, "You know there's an alley that runs behind the Santucci house. All the alleys have gates in the back for the trash containers."

"That's right," Cece said. "I imagine most people lock their back gates but if you were throwing something out, you could be in the alley at any time, day or night."

"What if Santucci confronted him out there?"

"Even if he did, do you think Fred could murder him? Bash him in the head and drag his body into the pond. That's a bit much. Fred looks like he couldn't trap a pack rat that had just chewed up the air conditioning cables in his car."

Stacey glanced at Cece and then down at Ollie B who was listening to their conversation intently. She shook her head at Cece, signaling "not now, later."

At that, Ollie B who had been quiet during their walk back to the car, piped in. "You really think he was murdered?" She looked inquiringly at her mother.

"No, no. Just a bad accident. People always wonder about that when there's an accident. You don't have to worry. The police will figure it out." She squeezed Ollie B's hand.

"The police should talk to us kids," Ollie B said with an emphatic nod. "We know more than people think. We know all the places in the alleys where anything can hide. All the places where the oleanders and bushes have pushed through the fences and walls. That's where we build our forts."

"What?" Stacey's eyebrows arched and her voice rose to a higher pitch. "You're going around the alleys? Ollie B, that could be dirty, not to mention dangerous. I didn't know you were playing there."

"It's okay, Mom. Don't have a cow! We don't do it at night, at least not us kids."

"Who *does* do it at night?" Stacey demanded, stopping abruptly to face Ollie B, hands on hips and face scrunched into a scowl.

Ollie B hung her head and muttered something indistinguishable.

"What was that?"

"Nothing." Ollie B pulled at her ponytail and chewed on the end. "I'm just saying, we think some of the older kids might hang out in some of the bigger places at night. Or …the boogyman," she added in a dropped voice. "Sally's big sister warned us not to go there or we'd be sorry. We sometimes see stuff, liquor bottles and things like that. So we're kind of scared."

"You should be."

Cece listened to this interchange with interest. First Crazy Carrie and now neighborhood hoodlums? The boogeyman? Did Encanto-Palmcroft have its own version of the Gilbert goons, privileged teenagers who think they can do whatever they want? Surely not. Encanto-Palmcroft wasn't that kind of place. Although what kind of place was the town of Gilbert? It was supposed to be one of the best suburban cities in the country to raise a family. What had gone wrong that it could foster such evil?

Maybe she should check out the alleys anyway. It never hurt to have more information. Thinking more about Gilbert and the goons who gang attacked random teen victims, Cece couldn't help but shudder. One thing seemed pretty obvious about the teen crimes in Gilbert—the kids knew. They videoed everything. It was the adults in charge who wouldn't listen. Shrugged it off…not enough information. Case closed. If Santucci was murdered, someone should be held accountable or what was the country coming to? If the police weren't interested, so be it. But this kind of thing could not happen in their neighborhood, Cece vowed. At least not without retribution. A little hike along the alleys of Encanto-Palmcroft seemed like a good next step. Intel gathering.

CHAPTER EIGHT

Five days after Santucci's death Brett Riley, the president of the Encanto-Palmcroft board, posted an announcement over the neighborhood email of Santucci's funeral. A vigil was being held Friday morning at St. Francis Catholic Church on 48th Street. Brett encouraged all from the neighborhood to pay their respects.

Cece read the announcement out loud to George as they were eating their breakfast. "What do you think? Should we go?"

George paused, chewing his toast thoughtfully before answering. "Not sure why we should go. It's not like we knew him. My brother did a little but that was decades ago. Not to mention that he was rude and nasty to us during the very short time we actually interacted with him."

"True enough." Cece finished up her cereal, swallowing the last spoonful of milk before adding, "But you know what they say about the funerals of murder victims."

George looked over at her, with a questioning frown. "No, what do they say?"

"They say," Cece paused to delicately wipe her mouth, "that the murderer can't resist attending. Just has to be there to appreciate the significance of his crime. Vanity, pure and simple."

"So they say that, do they? And who might those "they" be? Miss Marple, perchance!"

"Okay, smarty pants. For your information, yes, Miss Marple but others as well."

"Inspector Poirot? Or maybe the Pink Panther inspector? Clouseau, was that his name?"

"You don't have to come. I'll go and I bet some of the clubbers will go to. I've never been to St. Francis and I hear it's a beautiful church."

◆━━━━━◆≡◆━━━━━◆

The wake started at ten. Just as Cece anticipated, both Heidi and Anne wanted to go along. Stacey and Stephanie couldn't get out of work commitments.

"I haven't been to a wake before," Anne had said when they talked it over beforehand. "Do I have to wear a hat?"

"I didn't know either but I googled it," Cece had answered. "The answer seems to be 'no' since hats weren't mentioned in the list of suitable attire. Just dress conservatively and inconspicuously."

They arrived shortly after ten and entered the vestibule where a board stood by the entry. A large photo of Santucci was displayed prominently along with a number of other photos. A small group was milling around inside.

"Look for anyone who seems suspicious," Cece said.

"What would suspicious looks be? Or behavior? What exactly are we looking for?"

"We'll know it when we see it."

With a shrug Heidi followed Cece into the group of mourners. "People from his club, no doubt," Cece whispered, looking at the people around them. "Not sure he has any family members but when people start giving eulogies we'll have a better idea."

"Ha! Look what I see." Cece pointed across the room to a figure entirely shrouded in black, including a black hat and veil. "Could that be Dahlia? The bereaved Dahlia? Let's go by and pay our respects."

"The idea of dressing for a wake is to not stand out since the purpose of the wake is to support the family, not to show your personal grief," Cece whispered. "So there is Dahlia, not wearing bright yellow as usual but managing to stand out more than anyone else here."

Going up to Dahlia's turned back, Cece gently touched her shoulder. "Hi, Dahlia. I'm Cece. Remember me? We met briefly on Saturday in front of Sal's house. I'm sorry for your loss."

Dahlia gulped back a groan, dabbing her blue shaded eyes with a Kleenex. "Oh yes. I remember. It was so awful that morning! But then everything changed that afternoon. We reconciled, you know. After so long, we reconciled and we were going to be together. I was going to move in with him just next week. But now this," she wailed with a steadily rising voice. "How could this happen?" She looked to the ceiling as if the answer would be written across the rafters. "Why can't anything go right for me?"

Anne gave her a half hug and patted her back. "I'm sure there're answers. We have to have faith," she murmured uncertainly. She was going to say something about God's mysterious ways but decided against it.

At the side of the sanctuary they saw Brett Riley, dressed nicely in a dark suit and maroon tie. He looked quite debonair compared to his usual casual attire at neighborhood functions. He stood before the group and gave a short talk acknowledging Santucci's addition to the neighborhood and regretting how little time he had there to become acquainted with his new neighbors.

"That was nice," Cece commented when he finished.

"Harrumph," Dahlia snorted. "He's not important. He's not the one. It's her."

Cece glanced across the room, wondering who Dahlia was talking about. She noted a group of mourners talking solemnly together.

"She's the reason," Dahlia growled. "She thinks she owns him but I know better. He didn't care for her. He just used her."

Cece and Anne turned to follow the direction of Dahlia's stare. A youngish woman in somber clothes was dabbing her eyes with a sodden handkerchief. One of Santucci's strippers, no doubt, they both thought simultaneously.

When the young woman walked to the microphone and addressed the mourners, Dahlia's emotion was barely restrained. Her fists were clinched and she almost hissed a rebuke at her.

After the last words of her eulogy, Dahlia rose to the microphone. She looked around at the gatherers defiantly. "I've been with Sal since I was fifteen years old," she began, to the surprised looks of the assembled grievers. "Yes, longer than anyone and we were just beginning a new start to our lives." She paused to sob loudly into her Kleenex. "We were going to be together from now on, but now, now... He's gone. Taken from me," she cried in rising hysteria. She stepped down and hurried from the room, keening to the astonishment of all the onlookers.

Cece and Anne hurried out after her but by the time they emerged from the church, Dahlia was gone.

"Well, that was interesting," Cece said. "Last Saturday Santucci was screaming insults at her and now she claims they were together. Smell a rat?" she turned to Anne with a quizzical smile.

"Yes, I do. But let's go back in and hear the rest of the eulogies."

They returned in time to hear one of the speakers telling the story of the Santucci family. George was right, Cece thought. Santucci's family had been poor. His grandfather was a Sicilian stone mason, one of many who immigrated to Arizona in the early years of the twentieth century to help build Roosevelt Dam. At the time it was a monumental project, and one that changed the history of Phoenix forever. The intermittently running Salt River now had become a reliable source of water as well as a source of electricity for the newly growing community. Sal's parents had bought a home in Palmcroft and started a small pizza restaurant. It was hard to imagine a time when pizza was an unknown item to many American diners. Santucci had worked in his parents' restaurant after school and on weekends, so he had little time for the high school activities that consumed the popular kids. With his unattractive looks and social exclusion, no doubt Sal Santucci had an early life filled with unpleasantness.

"Not surprising that Santucci wanted to prove his success back in his old neighborhood where he was rejected as a kid," Cece whispered to Anne. She paused for a moment to scan the crowd more closely before adding, "Do you see anyone who looks like maybe family? Or an enemy?"

"Not so far," Anne answered.

They waited for a number of other speakers to present eulogies. But none seemed to be close to Santucci at a personal level. It seemed like they were all employees for his business,

Santucci Entertainment. Even a few other young women gave short speeches but all seemed impersonal.

As the wake was winding down and the attendees were drifting out, Cece motioned to Anne that they should go. Anne nodded back in agreement.

Once out of the church and heading back to the car, Cece sighed. "Not sure what we accomplished but it does seem like Santucci had no personal mourners there. No ex-wives, no children mourning the passing of a dad. Nothing but employees paying respects to their boss and getting a break in their work day. And most of all no one who looked nervous and suspicious. Even Dahlia just looked kind of crazy, not so much guilty."

"And probably most of them were mainly wondering what was going to happen to their jobs!"

CHAPTER NINE

Encanto-Palmcroft has more than three hundred houses, both large and small. Two circles encompass most of the southern end of Palmcroft, closest to the homeless camp at McDowell and Fifteenth Avenue. The houses inside the circle have wider front yards that narrow in the back to more like a point. Houses on the outside of the circles are the opposite. Narrower front yards but wide arching backyards.

At the curve of Palmcroft Way SW the long back fences and walls of several houses backed up to the vacant lot and adjoining park where the homeless camps were crowded under the trees at the very back edge of the vacant lot farthest from the streets but closer to the backyards of the homes. The owners of those homes were for obvious reasons the ones most concerned about the encampments. One of the homes had been vacant for a number of months as the owners had departed for a grand European tour.

Anne, who lived several homes away, had been keeping a wary eye on her neighbor's property while they were gone. She had not been in their backyard since the gate was locked and abundant vegetation obscured most of the view over the gate.

When Cece approached Anne with her idea of scouting the alleys, Anne was reluctant. "So now I'm your Watson, is that it?" she grumbled.

"No, no. We're partners in crime. Umm, that didn't sound right. We're partners in crime solving, is what I mean?"

"Does George know you're out doing all this snooping?" Anne tilted her head and squinted at Cece.

"No, not exactly because you know what he'd say. Right? He's a worrywart. Besides he has a heart condition. I have to keep unpleasant things away. He's prone to get overly upset at my goings on. So he knows but I make light of it, I guess you'd say. He makes fun of our snooping, so I let him tease me about it like it's no big deal." Cece smoothed down her sweater and smiled sweetly with her best imitation of the dutiful wife.

"Yeah, right." Anne couldn't help but laugh at her friend. "Stacey wants to come too and Ollie B even talked her into coming along as our scout. She's the one who says she knows where all the hideouts are. Too bad it's not still spring break. We'd have more time but in a way it doesn't matter because it's an afternoon and nighttime hangout so if we want to question anyone we've got to go when the kids are most likely to be around."

"That makes sense," Cece said. "Maybe we should make up a story about someone missing, something they wouldn't be involved in so they'll be more willing to talk about anything suspicious."

"Good idea. This calls for a cup of coffee and a bagel. Something I just happen to have."

After throwing around different ideas, they decided to say a friend of Ollie B's, just a kid like her but a little older, had a fight with her parents and had made good on a threat to run away. And now the parents are frantic to find her. The police wouldn't get involved until she was missing more than 48 hours because she's a teenager, not a really little kid. That was the story they planned to tell.

Cece asked, "Don't you feel a little guilty telling such a whopper of a lie?"

"Don't think so. Lying is the avenue of communication between parents and their teens. Ha, ha. More the norm, if anything."

"Okay, yes, I guess I can remember telling a few myself, not to mention my kids who were accomplished experts in the medium!" Cece laughed. They decided on the next afternoon to get started. After all, time was wasting.

Cece spent the day catching up on yard work. Her flower beds were finally starting to bloom. The petunias were in full bloom and snapdragons were budding. The early irises were sending up budding stalks. Roses, gaura, statice and alyssum were all in bloom. Such a glorious day, Cece thought, standing upright with a fistful of weeds. She admired her newly planted iris that she had dug up last fall from the garden of a friend who was moving back East. They were doing well, she was pleased to note. It was wonderful to have the city garden club virtually in her backyard. There were so many plant enthusiasts living nearby. She often helped out in the rose garden, pruning after the spring bloom and deadheading all summer. The garden club hosted many gardening groups. George was a member of the bonsai group that met monthly. Cece had thought about joining one of those groups but her gardening interests were eclectic. She loved the lushness of an English garden. She didn't really care what the plants were as long as they were bountiful and beautiful. So that favored annuals that didn't have to deal with the horrid summer desert heat.

She stood still, enjoying the quietness of the neighborhood. It was the middle of the city and the birds had the loudest voices she heard. Even the planes taking off and landing far to the south could not disrupt the birdsong and the beauty of the morning.

Cece pulled her sweater closer as a sudden breeze blew across her face somehow reminding her of problems lying ahead. I won't think about it all now. Surely there are no hoodlums, not to mention murderers in beautiful Palmcroft.

Shaking those unpleasant thoughts away, she looked down at her iris again. I think I'll pick out some more iris from our local expert's iris beds, she thought. Stanley Mortimer was a neighborhood legend for his hybridizing of prize winning iris. She definitely needed more iris, more perennials to appreciate for more than a season. The next garden club meeting would not be held for several months and Cece decided she would attend. It was such a plus to have the monthly Encanto-Palmcroft magazine to keep everyone informed on all the neighborhood activities.

Snapping herself back to the present, she thought of the expedition they had planned for five o'clock. Would it be just a wild goose chase or something else? You don't know if you don't try, she thought, brushing the dirt off the knees of her pants and throwing the weeds into the nearby trash container. It's funny how you can live in a neighborhood for years and never go in the alleys. Of course the homeowners whose yards abutted the alleys were responsible for keeping their sections cleared of trash and plant overgrowth. She wondered how many actually did that. Not sure that she would. It's hard to care as much about something you don't actually see and nobody associates with you.

The crock pot of stew was simmering along when Cece gathered up her purse and water bottle, clipped Nicky into his harness and headed for the front door.

"Be back soon." Cece called into George's study where she saw him at his drafting table absorbed in drawing plans for their supposed future getaway house. Busywork, she thought. Architects just never stop. When George was wrapped up in a design he might as well be on the moon for all he noticed what was going on around him. Very handy to be sure.

The afternoon was just beginning to fade into twilight. The days were definitely getting longer. When Cece reached Stacey's house, Anne was already there.

"Let's go." Stacey was gathering her things. "I need to get back before dark and I don't want Ollie B thinking she can wander around the alleys after dark." She cupped her hand around her mouth away from Ollie B's view. "She reads Nancy Drew and I'm afraid she's gotten wind of our sleuthing and wants to join in."

"That's amazing. I didn't know kids still read Nancy Drew."

"Yep."

"Okay, we'll play it down. Act like we're worried about the teenagers. We won't mention Santucci or his murder." Cece and the small group headed down the street.

"Have we definitely decided it's a murder?" Stacey whispered.

Anne rolled her eyes. "Don't know," she whispered back.

The nearest alley ran parallel to Ninth Avenue before bending west to cross Eleventh Avenue.

Ollie B charged ahead. "There's only one place here and it's not very big," she called back over her shoulder as she turned into the alley. She was literally bouncing with excitement.

"Hold your horses. We're coming."

Walking halfway down the block they came across a break in an old fence where an enclosure was made to hide the trash containers. The gate from the alley to the trash cans was overgrown with weeds and volunteer trees, pushing the cinderblock wall beyond to the breaking point.

"Nobody here," Ollie B announced after a quick look around. "I've seen kids here sometimes but it isn't really a good spot."

"Let's keep going. Where next?" Stacey looked at Ollie B.

They headed north across Palm Lane and into the larger lots of the Encanto neighborhood. Turning west, they entered the next alley. At the curve in the alley Ollie B pointed ahead to an overgrown tangle of branches growing almost horizontally from a chaste tree. The tree itself was almost unrecognizable because it was totally enveloped by a dense covering of cats claw vines. They approached slowly, trying to peer beneath the vines. A smothered giggle floated out. Success.

"Let me go in," Ollie B whispered. "They won't run if they see me, I think."

Stacey gulped. "OK, but I'm right here behind you and after

a minute we're all coming in."

Ollie B stooped to frog walk into a narrow space between the dense vines and the block wall. The ladies waited nervously. Less than a minute went by.

"That's long enough. I'm going in." Stacey stooped down and twisting her torso tried to squeeze in. She poked her head in but pulled out and turned to Anne. "Not enough room for us, I'm afraid."

After a couple of minutes Ollie B popped her head out. "I sort of know them. I'm giving them the spiel. Out in a sec."

A minute or two later Ollie B emerged. Dusting herself off, she said, "They're not much older than me so they don't really know anything. They haven't seen the ocelot but they heard about it, so they're pretty excited to see it. Pretty stupid, if you ask me! But they told me one thing that might be interesting. One of them has an older brother and she followed him one night to a hideout where she thinks they were getting booze. She ran away before her brother could see her but she's keeping it secret in case she needs to blackmail him some day."

"What??" Cece exclaimed. "Jeez, kids. What little manipulators!"

"Did she tell you where it is?"

"Of course. And I pretty much know where but I didn't know how it was being used. I thought it was one of those 'girls keep out' things that the boys do but I was wrong."

"Do we have time to find it?" Stacey glanced at the darkening sky.

Once she heard Ollie B describe the location of the other hideout, Anne gasped. "That sounds like the back of my neighbor's house, the neighbors who've been gone for the last three months. Can we make it over there in time?"

"Sure, if we hurry."

They made it to Palmcroft Way SW as fast as they could. The house was dark and even with a faint light within, it had an empty look. Nicky sniffed around finding nothing too exciting, so perked up his ears and waited for something to happen. Anne stared at the empty house. She was watching out for it. Surely nothing bad had happened. It was just an informal agreement. She didn't know the owners well and she didn't have a key for the house or the gate. "The only way to the back is along the alley. But it's open to the street and as we all know, it's also open to the homeless camp. Do we really want to go back there now in the almost dark?" She frowned at the thought.

They looked at each other and all shook their heads. "I need to take Ollie B home." Stacey looked at Ollie B. "I think we've done enough for today."

Everyone agreed, except Ollie B who looked totally ready to burst into the camp if given half a chance. Stacey pulled Ollie B's hand. "Let's disband and decide what to do tomorrow. And don't forget tomorrow is the schmooze. Let's think this over and meet there. Maddie might have some more information about the investigation. It would be good to have some idea what the police are thinking—and, hopefully, doing."

CHAPTER TEN

It was the third Sunday, the afternoon of the schmooze, just a week after the home tour and all of its excitement. George was settled into his favorite chair watching a basketball game. Cece looked over at him and queried, "I hope the basketball games aren't going to keep you from going to the schmooze this afternoon."

"Oh no. Another schmooze! During basketball season. What are they thinking?"

"I'm expecting you to show up for at least a little… or else."

George turned to frown at Cece. "Or else what?" He arched an eyebrow and lowered his head, suspiciously.

Cece leapt from her chair. "Or else this!" She pulled out an odd paper contraption that snapped at the end of her fingers. She jumped at George and poked him furiously, picking at his shirt.

"What are you doing?" He flung his arms over his chest in alarm.

"Cootie catcher, cootie catcher," Cece chanted, redoubling her attack.

"What! You crazy woman. Are you a third grader or what?" He swatted her off.

"Exactly. I'm channeling my third grade self and you're my victim. Ha!"

"I don't have any cooties so you can stop now, you nutcase."

Cece put down her cootie-catcher reluctantly. "Oh okay. You're no fun," she grumbled.

"Where'd you get that? I haven't seen a cootie-catcher in decades."

"Ollie B gave it to me yesterday when I was at Stacey's. I was so excited to see it, she thought I should have it. So here it is!" She held it up, snapping at the air with enthusiasm.

Nicky had bolted upright, watching this little drama with growing alarm. What now? he thought. Cooties? What were cooties? Maybe fleas. Biting bugs, eating at his furry body? His shaggy head flitted back and forth between George and Cece. Always something!

⋄───────⋄❈❖⋄───────⋄

The weather could not have been more perfect for an outdoor get together. Soft breezes through the budding elm trees, flowers bursting into bloom, everything that could be considered bucolic in the suburbs—such a tranquil setting in the midst of a gigantic city. Or, maybe not, Cece thought as she rousted George out of his tv chair.

"I hope you're coming with me this afternoon." Another attempt. She gave a determined scowl. "You need to get out and socialize. Doctor's orders as you well know."

George pulled himself out of his chair. "Okay, okay. I can do that. This game is almost over and it's not even a contest. Damn Suns. Why can't they ever win!"

"You need a break from worshipping at the church of the NBA. It's making you grumpy. Cheer up! We can take Nicky with us. He always cheers you up. It'll be contagious. He loves to walk and he even likes to socialize—more than you do." She looked down at Nicky who was at rigid attention, ears perked, body trembling in anticipation on hearing his favorite word "walk."

When George pulled on a sweater, Nicky whirled in excitement. "You forgot to spell that word, you know—w-a-l-k. You know he speaks English as well as dog. Won't be long before he can spell it too. Maybe we can use pig latin next."

"He's definitely a smart boy. What's his vocabulary now, do you think?"

"Probably 50 or 60 words at least. Plus he not only hears, he smells information a thousand times better than us poor humans."

Cece looked thoughtfully at Nicky. "You know dogs have more facial expressions than chimpanzees and they're the genetically closest animal to humans. Chimps that is, not dogs. But dogs are social animals like humans and for that reason must be able to communicate. To survive as a pack. I bet I could teach Nicky more words or concepts. Make motions like American Sign Language where actions are communicated rather than words. So I would run with him while saying 'run.' Or, I say 'run' and then we do it. We do that over and over with lots of treat rewards and I bet he'll learn in no time."

"Don't doubt it for a minute," George agreed. "If you want to do it, go for it, I say."

"Another thing that would help is to make the words always about something he cares about. I know from teaching reading to the grandkids that they learn the words quickly when they care about the story. So they have to be interested and the same would be true for Nicky."

"And what exactly is Nicky interested in?" George queried, raising an eyebrow.

"Hummm. Food, of course. Walks, other dogs and always cats. Sometimes people, at least when he first meets them. He scratches a bedding spot. So he cares about that. So I'm going to work on it."

"Good luck," George said. "We know for sure that he has a lot of emotion. You can see it in his eyes and especially in his ears."

George joined her at looking at Nicky. "I think a schnauzer cut makes his face even more expressive. Those silver eyebrows standing out, all fluffy-like and the silver whiskers making his smile or frown more exaggerated."

"And the shaved ears, making their movement more noticeable," Cece added. "I think you're right but I'm sure our boy knows a lot and tries to tell us what he knows. He must be pretty frustrated with us dense humans!"

After a moment Cece added, "Another reason we should be able to communicate better is because dogs and humans have evolved together over the last thousands of years. Here in North America dogs were the only domesticated animal until the Spanish arrived in the sixteenth century. The domesticated alpaca and llama of South America could not breach the tropics of the isthmus of Panama to ever make it to Mexico or America. So we humans have a long history with dogs. However dogs process communication more slowly than humans so I need to speak slowly to Nicky."

While Cece and George were discussing Nicky's communication skills, Nicky was waiting patiently or as patiently as possible when he knew he was about to go on a walk. He looked up at his two human companions. Indeed he was very fond of them, amazingly so. After all they were the center of his existence quite literally. He did though wish they were a little smarter, more perceptive. He sighed and rested his head on his crossed front paws and waited.

The five or six blocks to the Henderson schmooze was leisurely with many stops for Nicky to sniff every palm tree trunk, lamp post and bush along the way.

"Doggie internet," Cece mused.

George laughed. "Or maybe peemail. This boy leaves lots of posts. He's on LegBook. He's got a lot to say, I think."

"What do you think he learns with all this sniffing?"

"Who's on the streets, maybe their health, their state of mind, what they're planning, good or bad."

"Hummm. I think you're right. He knows much more than we used to think. Wouldn't you love to know what's going through his mind?" Cece watched lovingly as Nicky continued about his business presumably unaware of his humans' ruminations.

"Maybe not. We'd have a window into everybody in the neighborhood. TMI if you ask me! What if he knows too much about us humans as well as the animal life? That might be disturbing."

It wasn't long before they crossed the street and approached Encanto Drive. Grassy front lawns graced the notable grand houses that lined the drive. Upstairs balconies, gracious front patios, fire pits—all the accoutrements for a happy life, Cece thought. She laughed at herself. She sounded like those fluffed up home descriptions in a real estate listing. Down the street they passed a beautiful home once owned by the daughter of Franklin Roosevelt. Barry Goldwater had lived nearby. A beautiful place for sure but what secrets did it also hold? Was there a dark underbelly for Encanto-Palmcroft? She inwardly shuddered.

Once they arrived at their hosts' front patio, Cece settled into a comfortable Adirondack lawn chair with a glass of chardonnay and surveyed the scene before her, thinking of the alleys of the evening before.

Nicky scurried under her chair where he held a wide observation post for all that was going on. Crossing his front paws, he laid his head down and enjoyed the spectacle as well. But mainly Nicky was focused on the myriad of smells. The turbid mix of giddy joy, hidden anxiety, incipient illness and a host of other less definable conditions. Nicky enjoyed the wild array of smells rising and settling over the yards and alleyways as the breezes wafted the evidence of people, animals, cars and the constantly changing landscape. Nicky tilted his head, raising an ear into a slight breeze that rumpled the grass around the chair.

There was that smell again—cat—but not quite cat. Something more, something feral, dangerous. Not the scent of cat food and milk, more like rat guts! Nicky shuddered once but then forgot. Too many other goings on to let his mind be still. He was not one to dwell on the negative!

Fifty or more people had already gathered, groups forming and shifting into new groups. Cece scanned the crowd more closely and caught sight of Maddie coming around the street corner and heading her way. Heidi was right behind her. Cece stood up to wave them over.

Breathless, Maddie, definitely in a hurry, rushed up and smiled a greeting. Hardly catching her breath, she said, "I'm getting something to drink. Be right back. I'll get you something too, Heidi. Tell them what happened this morning." She turned and disappeared into the crowd milling around the drinks and snacks tables.

All eyes zeroed in on Heidi. "I'll wait for Anne. I see her parking her car over there." She nodded toward the far sidewalk.

"Jeez! Don't keep us in suspense. What is going on?" Cece was practically jumping from foot to foot although still seated!

CHAPTER ELEVEN

Finally, drinks in hand, Anne and everyone settled into chairs, leaning forward in anticipation. Maddie had returned and she started first. "Ok, here's the latest. On Friday the detectives on the Santucci case were finishing up their interviewing. Apparently they were focused on Dahlia but were lacking enough evidence to tie her to Santucci's death. Obviously, just anger at him is hardly damning enough evidence of a crime. Half of Encanto-Palmcroft probably didn't like him, as well as who knows how many others. Being a mobster isn't a winning occupation for getting any 'most popular' awards. Anyway, the autopsy has not been released but the word is there isn't anything incriminating in it. Only that he had a .19 blood alcohol level. Very drunk. So they're still thinking it's possible the poor sot just did himself in through drunken carelessness. The time of death has been narrowed down to between 11:00 p.m. Saturday and 3:00 a.m. Sunday morning. The timing is a little more difficult with a submerged body. They've interviewed all the—ahem—guests at his pool party that night and they all said he was downing booze like it was water. Even his strippers were pretty much done with him. So no evidence of foul play on their part. They claimed they had all left before midnight and he was alive then and they're backing each other up. So it looks like he probably died around one or two a.m. That's where things were until this morning." She paused and shifted to nod at Heidi who had drawn up a chair on her right. "Go on, Heidi. Tell them the rest."

Heidi started, a little breathless. "I was barely out of bed this morning when the police knocked on my door. Well, not the police, two detectives. I can tell you that brings a sense of dread. They flashed their badges and said they wanted to talk to my son! You all know Ryan. I had to roust him out of bed. He's only sixteen and you know how teenagers are with sleeping in. I had to half drag him out of bed. He came down the stairs looking pretty wretched, with Hector—y'all know how he gets—right behind him as if he had a whip and was ready to use it.

"It was Detective Fotinus and the other guy, Miller, I think. So, Fotinus started grilling Ryan about his whereabouts on the night before the home tour. Last Saturday night a week ago when Santucci died. I was scared half to death that they thought Ryan had somehow had something to do with it but that wasn't exactly it. Fotinus was investigating the charge that Ryan and a few of his buddies were out that night at the homeless camp and dealing drugs— meth, cocaine, heroin, I don't know what all. Believe me, his father and I were totally freaking out. Ryan looked so scared and… so young—my baby." Heidi paused to catch her breath. She shuddered, the memory bringing a look of disbelief that rippled across her forehead.

"Ryan swore he wasn't at the camp and had nothing to do with any drugs, but Fotinus kept pressuring, badgering him. Hector got so mad he was about to kick him out and get an attorney when Ryan kind of broke down and said he'd tell him what happened that night.

"He said his friends wanted to go to the homeless camp to find some drifter named Lucky who was known to live there off and on. He was mainly known for drug dealing but he'd also go to the Seven Eleven just across the street on McDowell and buy beer for the underage kids for a fee. That's what the boys wanted. A six pack. Ryan didn't want to do it, he swore. He had other plans and, besides, he thought the camp was too scary but he didn't want to admit that to his friends. He told his buddies his other plans were a secret."

The women were gathered around Heidi, silent and listening intently. Heidi shifted in her chair, eyes blinking as if it had all been a bad dream. She continued. "So Ryan split off and headed north into the alley behind the Santucci house. He told us that there were rumors that Santucci was having a pool party with a lot of the strippers who worked his Scottsdale club. Ryan's plan was to secretly video the strippers. He thought they'd probably be naked or close to it. If he got some good pics, he could post them on social media or maybe even sell them."

Heidi shook her head dejectedly. "Damn kids, don't have a brain in their heads. I couldn't believe he would want to do such a thing."

Stephanie, the high school counselor, patted her knee sympathetically, nodding her head. "Don't be too upset. They're just boys showing off. Not too unusual."

"Thanks, Stephanie, I know but still. That's what he said he wanted to do. So when he got to the back of Santucci's property, he realized the party seemed to be winding down and there was arguing going on. Some of the women sounded like they were leaving, angry at Santucci and shouting at him. Sounded like maybe he was drunkenly trying to grope some of them. Ryan listened from behind the back wall but still wanted some photos before the strippers left and it was too late. He shinnied up some trees growing against the wall and just as he got high enough and was ready to film he heard someone coming up behind him from the alley. He flattened himself against the wall and the branches pretty much covered him from view. He looked out between the limbs and saw a woman approaching. She had a cell phone. It was in a shiny yellow case, he noticed. She opened Santucci's gate a crack and looked in, holding her phone up. She looked like she was filming what was going on inside.

"He watched her slip through the opening but just then Ryan heard a weird noise, a low growl, coming from above him. He looked up. He saw two bright orange glowing eyes reflecting the moonlight— a dark shadowy form with black splotches. Some kind of creature was crouched in the branches of a big tree that hung over the wall just above him. He was terrified. He said he thought it was a tiger or a jaguar or something and he just jumped down and ran as fast as he could home. He thought it was chasing him. He jumped in bed, covered himself with quilts and shook in fear the whole night. He never said a word about any of it later. So all this was going on and us, his naive parents, had no idea!" Heidi's shoulders slumped. "It was probably the ocelot. Escaped but still in Santucci's yard, loose. Ryan didn't even know about it. These kids, so wrapped up in social media and their own lives, they don't even know what's going on around them. It's not like it hasn't been news. And we thought he was always so open with us. Told us everything. We've actually bragged about that!" she continued as the group edged closer in rapt attention.

"Anyway, Fotinus asked him to describe the woman and Ryan said he didn't get too good a look at her but she was wearing a bright yellow sweater. He remembered that because he thought it was pretty dumb of her if she was going to be sneaking around. He had made sure he was wearing all black." Heidi shook her head again, as if it were impossible for her son to be that sneakily clever. "She had blonde hair that picked up the moonlight and big—he didn't want to say it—but Fotinus waited until he admitted—big boobs. He's a boy, sixteen. So I guess you're right, Stephanie, it's not too surprising. He did notice something else though and that proved pretty important. He said she waited at the gate before she opened it to pull a stick of gum out of her pocket. She popped it into her mouth and dropped the wrapper on the ground. Fotinus got pretty excited by that because a Juicy Fruit wrapper had been picked up by the crime scene investigators who searched the whole area after Santucci's body was found. That helped give credibility to Ryan's account of what happened."

"So obviously Dahlia," they all nodded and couldn't help but look across to the far end of the lawn where Dahlia was chatting up some man with his back turned to them.

"So what does that all mean?" the women chorused.

Maddie broke in, "There's a rumor that they are closing in on the investigation, that they have a viable suspect. So it looks bad for Dahlia. Now there's a witness that puts her at the scene of the crime, within the time frame of the death and with a powerful motive. They might get a fingerprint match from the gum wrapper. The fact that he was so drunk makes it more likely that a woman could have had the strength to commit murder."

At the word "murder" they all sat still, stunned into silence.

"Wow! When will Fotinus act, do you think?" Cece leaned forward in her chair, eyes wide.

Heidi shook her head and sighed. "Fotinus shut down and wouldn't say a word. I badgered him. Like would Ryan have to testify in a trial? Was he still in trouble? Fotinus wouldn't respond, said we had to wait. It was pretty clear, we thought, that he had come to the house about the drugs at the homeless shelter and everything that Ryan told him was new information. He seemed pretty excited when he realized that he was on to something much more important. He just told us to stay in town and make sure that Ryan was available for further questioning if necessary. I asked if Ryan was in any kind of danger but he wouldn't answer directly. Just said not to worry. Right!! Not worry, sure. My son's a witness in a murder case. The murder of a mobster most likely. What's to worry about?" she exclaimed, wringing her hands and taking a big gulp from her wine glass.

Solemn nods all around.

Cece turned to Maddie. "I don't think the police can now say there's not enough evidence. This makes murder a far more likely explanation than an accident. What on earth was Dahlia thinking, going to his house in the middle of the night to spy on him? Did she think she could get some dirt on him to make him mad? Some kind of revenge?"

"Maybe he attacked her and she was just defending herself." Maddie shrugged. "That seems to be the usual defense when no one's around to witness what happened," she added.

They all nodded agreement.

"But really. What if they got in a fight, pushing and that sort of thing. And Santucci staggered back and tripped over the edge of the pond and fell into it hitting his head on the far edge.

If he was knocked out plus plastered he probably could drown. Would that be murder? I don't think so. But she was a stripper. That will cause bias against her."

Cece held out her hand palm up. "Hold on, I saw the body, remember, and if what you suggested happened, that he fell backwards into the pond, he would have been face up in the pond. And he wasn't. Very much face down."

"Humm, ok that is different. To be face down he would have had to be in front of the pond, facing it and fallen forwards, hit his head on the far edge and then slipped down into the water."

"She could have come up behind him when his back was turned and pushed him hard so he toppled forward."

"Or maybe he just fell on his own," Cece added and they nodded. "So where are we? Is it definitely murder or not? I really wish we knew what the police are thinking. Anyway if they do bring charges, I think she'd have a pretty good defense if she had a good attorney."

"Does she have the money for that?" Anne queried.

They all shrugged.

"She certainly behaves like a gold digger, you know, like she's desperate for a man. Or maybe it's money she's desperate for and men are the means to access that. Maybe she is really hurting for money. She wouldn't be the first. Almost makes me feel sorry for her."

"Humph," Anne snorted. "If your career goals depend on your looks then you better know you're not going to fair too well when you could be a grandma pushing sixty."

"Couldn't deny that!" They all nodded.

Maddie broke in. "I'll keep my eyes open at the courthouse and see what I can find out. Let you all know as soon as I get wind of anything."

With that, the group broke up, scattering to find their partners and gathering up their leftover bottles to take home. Cece spotted George across the lawn, talking to a group of men. She sidled over, pulling Nicky behind her. He was digging in his paws, not wanting to go but George was ready. As they walked across the yard to the street, they passed near Dahlia chatting up poor Stanley Mortimer, the iris grower. Cece had to pull Nicky's leash to keep him going. He had stiffened and let out a low growl, digging his paws into the soft grassy lawn. "Come on, Nick," Cece urged, pulling harder until he gave up and trotted along reluctantly.

As they approached the sidewalk Cece looked over her shoulder, getting a last glimpse of that bright yellow dress. Dahlia! It looked like she had poor Stanley Mortimer cornered, standing close to him, smiling a broad coy smile up into his face. He looked decidedly uncomfortable, his big loose-limbed body sloughing back to distance himself from her, Cece thought. She never gives up the man hunt. No widower would be safe from her. Cece chided herself. Be kind! Despite Dahlia's showy social presence at all their neighborhood events, blatant man chasing and so many selfies on Facebook, she seemed fundamentally lonely. Was it her own fault or were there other forces at work that Cece could never know about? With that thought, Cece decided she would just wait and see. But a feeling of unease made her wonder, what did Nicky sense? Dahlia virtually reeked phoniness. Nicky could read people in ways we couldn't. He was on to something. That she was sure of.

CHAPTER TWELVE

Monday morning dawned springlike beautiful and the garden was calling. When the garden calls, Cece responds, or so she thought. So there she was kneeling in the cool grass in her front garden pulling the weeds that had popped up after the recent downpour. She knew water was a problem in a desert environment but what a pleasure to sit on real grass and not the ubiquitous rocks of so many other Phoenix neighborhoods. She was totally in a weed-pulling zone, oblivious to the world of commuter cars on nearby I-10, the faint drone of planes landing at Sky Harbor and the whistles of the freight trains heading northwest along Grand Avenue on their way to California.

Then Heidi jogged by. "Hey," Heidi called out, spotting Cece.

Cece looked up, snapping into the present and recognizing her friend. "Any news?" She got up, dusting the dirt off her hands and her gardening pants and looked at Heidi expectantly.

"Aren't you the anxious one. It's only Monday morning so not yet as far as I know. Too soon. Maybe Maddie will have something for us later."

"True enough. How's Ryan doing? I imagine being grilled by the cops was pretty unsettling."

"Probably more to me and Hector than to Ryan. Now that he's had time to think about it I get the feeling he thinks he might be a big shot. You know, witnessing a maybe murder. Plus of course being in the bleachers to a stripper fracas."

"I bet." Cece laughed. "Nothing like a little teenage imagination to create a whole new story!"

"Still we've warned him to not talk about it. I am worried. Who knows what kind of criminals Santucci and his stripper girls are involved with. But one thing is good about the whole incident. Ryan's seeing the gum wrapper that the woman dropped proved that he was there and not at the homeless camp getting illegal beer. Plus the others boys ran for it when they saw the cops coming so it now looks like that investigation is going nowhere at least for now."

"Good. That's that." Cece nodded her head. High jinks. Hadn't they all done a bit as teens.

"Not to change the subject but I've been thinking about the so-called creature Ryan saw that night. It had to have been the ocelot even though Ryan thought it was big like a mountain lion. But that's fear adrenaline I think exaggerating his vision. So we don't know when it escaped or was released but apparently it didn't take off at least right away. I know Fred is really worried about it. This isn't their native habitat never mind that it's a giant city with so many dangers. I think we should let him know that Ryan saw it. It suggests that the ocelot is a female and may stick around."

"I sure wouldn't mind going over to his place. I'd love to see it again. When I saw it on the last home tour Fred wasn't around so there really wasn't anyone who could answer all my questions about his plants."

"I have an open house I have to sit at so I won't be available until around four. What do you think? Want to go over then?"

"Sure. Shouldn't we call him first?"

"Yes, of course, but I don't hold out much hope that he'll answer. He's notoriously introverted. So if we just show up he might talk to us. He does love his little wildlife sanctuary and likes to talk about it if you get him going. Otherwise he's pretty darned withdrawn. He seems to be a nice guy, just a little odd."

"Aren't we all," Cece sighed.

"Ha! Speak for yourself!"

"Like I said. I called but it went to voicemail. Anyway here we are." Heidi and Cece had walked over to Fred's house and now Heidi had raised a fist to knock on the weathered wooden front door. Silence. She knocked again. "What should we do? Coming here probably wasn't a good idea."

Cece looked around the abundant plantings virtually smothering the entire front yard. "Let's not give up too soon. We can poke around and see if we spot him. With a yard like this he probably spends every second tending to it."

"Yeah. It looks like a lot of work."

A narrow pebble path wound from the small front porch around the side yard to the garage area. A large planting bed covered the space between the garage and the side fence. As they approached, Cece bent down to investigate more closely the tangle of flowers, shrubs and bushes. What on earth was he growing? Plumeria and maybe brugmansia, the very poisonous angel's trumpet! The tropics in the desert. Add water to the desert and what do you have! Cece thought. The jungle!

Just then a head popped up from behind a thicket of cats claw vines covering a wooden cage. Fred! He scowled at them as if they were burglars.

"Hi, Fred," Heidi gulped and stammered, "We've got, er, some news… we thought you might want to know."

Fred said nothing. He continued to eye them, brow creased and shoulders hunched forward as if he might lunge at them at any moment. His more or less friendly demeanor at the wildlife center had vanished and was replaced by a much more enigmatic expression. He tottered unsteadily before righting himself. He pushed down his shirt sleeves to cover his dirty, bandaged arms.

"Remember me from Liberty? We brought the kids' club donation from their home tour lemonade stand. We chatted a bit there," Cece added hopefully.

Fred sighed, his shoulders lowered and the wrinkled forehead smoothed.

Cece sighed also, the relief contagious.

"I wasn't expecting anyone," Fred murmured.

"We're sorry to bother you but we thought you might want to know there was a spotting of the ocelot from Santucci's house."

At that Fred's face transformed, the usual gloom of his features brightening. "When? Where?"

"Unfortunately it was the night Santucci died, so more than a week ago. But still the ocelot was seen in a tree overlooking the alley behind his house. So we don't know when it was freed but at midnight it had not run off. It was sticking close to its home base."

"I knew it," he muttered to himself. "It's a female." With that he seemed to withdraw, going into his inner thoughts seemingly oblivious to the women.

Cece and Heidi stood there, shifting their weight uncomfortably. "We'll let you get back to your work," Heidi volunteered. "We thought you would want to know," she repeated awkwardly.

"Yes, yes," he said with an undercurrent of anger resurfacing. Then he seemed to forget they were there.

"Well, so long. Nice seeing you again. We certainly hope the ocelot is safe and can be recaptured." Cece sighed, turning and pulling Heidi along.

On the drive home, Heidi asked, "What do you think?"

"He's an odd one alright. He seems so harmless. It's hard to imagine that he had a shouting match with Santucci after the last board meeting. But there were a lot of witnesses so it had to have happened."

"I know. Hard to picture that going on. But isn't it always the quiet loner misfits who go berserk and shoot up a school or something?" Heidi shivered. "Do you think he could have released the ocelot?"

"I don't know." Cece shook her head in frustration. "Why would he release the ocelot if it would obviously escape and then be seriously endangered. Wild animals that turn up in civilization usually don't fare too well."

"That's for sure," Heidi agreed. "Plus she was a captive. She might have never learned to hunt. She could starve."

"But there are food supplies. Think of the pigeons. And the garbage cans out on the street every Tuesday. That's like an animal lunch cart."

"What if Fred tried to take her, but she got away from him?" Heidi asked and then hesitated abruptly. "Wait, did you see his arms? Those bandages?"

"Yeah. I did see them. And he seemed like he hurried to cover his arms. Wild animals in captivity are not necessarily tame. Probably never are. If he tried to take her, she would have fought him, don't you think? Fred looked pretty damn nervous the whole time we were there."

They sat in the car in front of Cece's house and contemplated the encounter.

"I can't help but feel he's involved. He obviously doesn't want us to know. He wouldn't admit it. It would be burglary. I bet ocelots are expensive. The illegal exotic animal trade is no doubt a million dollar enterprise or more." Heidi turned to Cece. "So now what?"

"We wait. I bet she's spotted soon. I just hope she isn't hit by a car or cornered in a tree or somewhere and the police come in and shoot her as a danger to humans."

"It's us humans who are the danger," Cece said, opening the car door. She turned back to Heidi, adding, "Any living thing that can't accommodate *our* lives, we pretty successfully eliminate."

"Except coyotes. They're the ultimate survivors. They'll outlast us for sure!"

"Coyotes and cockroaches."

CHAPTER THIRTEEN

"Emergency meeting, book club. My house, four o'clock. Come if you can. You won't believe it!!!"

Cece got Maddie's text at two-thirty. What now? she wondered with more than a little anticipation. An hour and a half. I can't stand it. What is going on?? Cece pondered how much of their snooping around she should tell George about. He was so content to tinker with endless designs—a house to maybe build, not to mention chairs, tables, endless furniture that of course if ever built would have no place to house them. They were full to the gills with a lifetime of collected stuff. And like most Americans, a garage at least half full as well. It's all about keeping productive, Cece thought. Or at least the illusion of productivity. And probably that applied to both of them, just in different contexts.

"George, I'll be over at Maddie's for a little. Back by dinner. It's your turn to cook, right?" She of course knew it was but that was just a little reminder in case she didn't make it back by dinnertime. Since she had no idea what was going on, it was best to make sure to not be hemmed in time-wise by annoying domestic duties.

She heard a muffled harrumph indicating "yes" from the inner sanctum of George's study. So that was taken care of.

She slipped on a light jacket against the cooling early April late afternoon and headed for the front door. A little body was parked in her way, blocking the door. "Sorry, Nicky." She looked guiltily at his expectant furry face, upturned in her direction. "I can't take you this time. You need to stay home and guard the home front. There are definitely forces of darkness to watch out for and no one can do that better than you. Your ole Daddy needs you. Right??"

Nicky wasn't buying it. He flattened his ears and grumbled a throaty complaint. How could she leave him now? He knew something was up. He could smell the excitement and anticipation in her every move. Why didn't she realize he could figure it all out. He could smell it!! And besides he still wanted to see Daisy, even if she did fall asleep and ignore him. No use. The door closed quietly in his face. What he had to put up with—with the two-legged. Can't live with 'em, can't live without 'em!

Cece pulled up to Maddie's curb just as Heidi and Anne were walking up the sidewalk. Once inside, Maddie set out a tray of snacks and glasses and a pitcher of fresh squeezed lemonade. She turned and motioned, "Dig in. I have news. It just traveled around the court house gossip circuit after lunch. Late this morning Detectives Fotinus and Miller went to pick up Dahlia. I don't know for sure if it was for more questioning or with an indictment. There's disagreement about that. But it doesn't matter because when they got to her house and banged on the door, she wasn't answering. They saw her car so they were pretty sure she was there. They thought maybe she was hiding, like she thought it might be a summons. So instead of leaving to get a warrant they went around back to check the backyard. There was an old garage separate from the house and when they forced the side door open, they found her. Dead!"

Everyone gasped, clutching their glasses and sloshing lemonade over the edges.

"Hanged from the rafters."

"Oh my gosh!" They all sat silently for a moment, overcome by the thought of such a terrible act. Soon their questions started and they began overtalking each other.

"Let me finish," Maddie exclaimed, picking up her glass and waving it around in an attempt to quiet them down.

"Yes, yes," they chorused.

"So they got her down, called an ambulance and the crime scene techs. Everything is probably yellow taped off by now."

"Let's get over there," Heidi interrupted. "Maybe there's still time to find out more."

They all agreed and piled into Heidi's big "real estate lady" SUV and headed south across McDowell and into the Story neighborhood. A few blocks down they saw obvious crime scene activity. Maddie parked a half block away and they funneled out and hurried down the street toward the milling police, techs and nosy neighbors kept at bay behind the yellow tape that was now strung across the front yard from the fence to the hedge that surrounded the little blue bungalow.

"What happened?" Cece asked the nearest grey-haired lady who was leaning over the tape like she was contemplating a high jump.

"It's that woman, the old…er, er."

"Exotic dancer," her nearby companion piped in. "A stripper," she added waggling her sparse eyebrows suggestively. "If you know what I mean?"

Cece couldn't help but smile. Dahlia wanted to be noticed and that she was. Just not always the way she probably thought.

"They just wheeled her out a little while ago," the old lady added. "She was covered of course so we couldn't see her. But everybody now knows she was hanged."

"Who said that?" Cece wondered aloud.

"Don't know. It's just going around. Like I said people around here all know who she is even if they don't actually know her. Who she was, that is. She was always out and about. Telling everyone how she hated that strip club owner, the guy with the big house in Encanto. She said he was her fiancee but she dumped him because he's a crook and a cheat. Was, that is. Was a crook. He's dead too!" She frowned as the reality of death must have just jolted her thoughts.

Cece turned in time to see Maddie sliding between the onlookers and up to the tape. She called to one of the crime scene techs who came over to her side. Obviously someone she knew. Cece threaded her way through the crowd to join Maddie. She stood by quietly to hear their conversation.

"Any note? Anything?"

The tech was young with a short dark beard to match his dark eyes. And a physique that his coveralls definitely could not disguise. A good looking guy, just the type Maddie would attract, Cece thought. He shrugged, "Can't say." Then he leaned closer and whispered by her ear. "Just one word, 'Sorry.'"

Maddie was their best asset for information gathering. That was for sure.

"Nothing more, yet. We'll be here for a while."

Maddie pulled Cece over to her side. "Let's round everyone

up and head back. We're not going to find out anything now. And it's getting late and I'm starved."

With everyone back in the SUV, they headed north for the short drive back to their neighborhood. The iconic lamp posts of Palmcroft were pinging on as the day darkened, giving the streets a mellow ambiance, calm and serene. But murder? Here? And now suicide just blocks away? But was it murder? And was it suicide?

"I'm sure I'll find out a lot more tomorrow. So do you all want to try to get together after dinner then? Seven as usual?"

They all chimed with agreement. Maddie's tomorrow at seven.

CHAPTER FOURTEEN

Cece texted Heidi. That was the great thing about real estate. A lot of hard work but often you could adjust your schedule if you needed to. And Heidi was a master at that! Anne worked from home and could sometimes find quite amazing flexibility in her schedule but she couldn't count on it. Stephanie was at West High until four so she was out for a morning excursion. So Heidi it was.

Cece and Heidi drove back to Story and parked near Dahlia's house. The street was quiet. Most of the residents had already left for work. Kids were in school. The yellow tape was still in place but there was no one around. Cece noted a dog walker who headed across the street to gape at the house, but really there was nothing to see. No burned out house, no blood splotches on the sidewalk. Nothing. The dog walker soon moved on.

Cece sent a quick text to Maddie, hoping she was free to respond. But a court reporter is only free when she's not in the courtroom and Maddie didn't respond.

Heidi looked around carefully. "No one's out. Let's make it quick and get under the tape." They slid under only barely threatening to drag it down when it caught on Cece's jacket collar. "That was good." Heidi dusted off her hands, looked around again. No one in sight so they headed for the backyard.

When they reached the dilapidated garage, they stared. In the bright light of morning, it looked more like a shed than a real garage. The gravel driveway was overgrown with weeds like it hadn't been used in years.

"That was built way before automatic garage doors, that's for sure." Cece pulled at the sagging side door. It opened with a little extra effort and they entered. A musty smell invaded their nostrils.

"What smells so bad?" Heidi coughed.

"Rat pee."

Heidi's brow furled. "Good to know. Ugh! So what are we looking for anyway?"

"Clues, of course. Was this really a suicide? Do you think Dahlia was that desperate?"

"Was she capable of doing herself in? She was a narcissist for sure. If you're so in love with yourself, how could you then kill yourself?"

"Good question." Cece scratched her chin. "If you're about to be exposed as a murderer and know you're going to prison, I think that might be sufficient."

"It's such an act of desperation. On the surface Dahlia seemed quite genuinely pleased with herself. I bet she thought her—assets," Heidi made "air quotes" around the word—"would always work for her. Don't think she really saw herself as over the hill. Probably photoshopped her selfies on Facebook and fooled herself into thinking she was still a big sexpot."

"Don't you think we all do that a little?" Cece mused.

Heidi shook her head chuckling. "Speak for yourself." She

paused. "Haven't I just said that to you recently?"

"Yes, but we all see ourselves as maybe better than we really look but I'm not so sure we think we're big sex symbols."

"That's for sure." Cece looked around in silence for a moment. "You know I read once that women who expose themselves to get attention were often victims of sexual abuse when they were young. Like all they know about their power in the world is linked to being sexy. That's just so sad. Such a tragedy for any young girl. So who knows with Dahlia. Maybe that was her background. What a depressing idea and this is a depressing place. I think I'd off myself if I had to spend much time here."

"Oh, I don't think so." Heidi scanned the small room, dirt floor and wooden walls. "I think it would make a great she-shed! I can just picture it with beaded curtains, pillows on the floor and good music."

"Ha, you're channeling your inner hippie." Cece looked closer, running her eyes up and down the aged wooden walls. "You do have a point. Cleaned up and with a window clean enough to actually let in light, it might be pretty cute. That's why you're the Realtor and I'm not. You can find the potential anywhere, which I must say is a great talent!"

"Despite all that *kumbaya*, remember a woman died here. So for now it's darn creepy." Heidi started walking around the perimeter of the area. "Why isn't there a chair or a stool here. Don't you have to kick one out from under you in order to hang yourself?"

"Guess so. The techs could have taken things out. Or the police. What if it wasn't suicide? What if someone murdered her and made it look like suicide. If it looked like she was going down for murdering Santucci, maybe someone wanted revenge.

Like to avenge his murder."

"Yeah, maybe, but it doesn't seem like anyone liked Santucci enough to want revenge. George told me he was bullied in high school and generally tormented because his parents were poor Sicilian immigrants and he was a short chubby geeky kid."

"Kids can be cruel. They were then and I suppose a lot still are. But someone must have cared for him, maybe?" Heidi arched her brows quizzically.

"Here's another idea. What if Dahlia really had managed to get herself on the title of Santucci's house? That's what she said she had done but nobody believed her since obviously she wasn't living there and Santucci totally shunned her. But if she had a claim, the house could have gone to her once Santucci died. And if that happened where would it go if Dahlia died?"

"Huh, you are quite the sleuth. So, yes, Dahlia might have had a good motive to murder Santucci but who would have a motive to kill her? Santucci was the only one known to despise her and he's dead so unless his ghost did it, he's in the clear."

"Let's get in the house if we can. Maybe we can find something there." Cece opened the garage door and headed for the back of the house. It didn't take long before they found a window stuck closed by years of disuse and multiple layers of paint.

"These old metal crank windows. Once the inside crank breaks off, there's no way to close them properly. I think I can pry it open."

"I saw some tools in the garage. Let's find a pry bar or something like that."

They headed back to the garage where it didn't take long to find a small pry bar sufficient for the job. Back at the window Heidi began hacking away layers of paint that stuck the panes to the steel frame.

"Yep. I still have some of these windows in my house. After almost a hundred years you're lucky if any of them work. Besides they're single paned so not so great for keeping the heat out. But you'd think they were treasures if you ask the historic preservation people. Try replacing them, in the front of your house at least, and see the hassle you get."

Heidi worked her fingers behind a corner of the window pane and tugged. "Fortunately whoever owned this house didn't bother to modernize. I think we're in!" The window pulled loose. The panes were just wide enough to crawl through.

Heidi looked at the narrow opening dubiously, "You first."

"No, you. You're smaller. You didn't manage to pack on the pounds this winter like the rest of us."

"Ok, ok, but…" Heidi turned to face Cece. "I'm pretty sure this would be considered breaking and entering."

"No it's not. We're not breaking anything. Just entering. So what's the crime there? We're friends of Dahlia, aren't we?"

"Sure, if you say so." She shook her head ruefully. "Beam me up."

Cece cupped her hands low for Heidi's tennis shoe and hoisted her up and into the window as far as her waist.

"Jeez. I'm stuck. Push." Heidi wiggled and squirmed her way through the window. "I'm in," she grunted. Pulling herself all the way through, she dropped down onto a bed pushed against the wall. That was handy. Thank goodness for over furnished rooms, she thought as she scanned the small bedroom she had dropped in to. She turned back to Cece on the other side of the window. "I'll go to the back door and see if I can open it."

Soon they were both in, scouting the house. The rooms were

small but fully furnished. Lots of framed photos of show girls and Vegas clubs lined the walls.

"That must be Dahlia in an earlier life." Heidi pointed to a photo of a much younger woman, costumed in pink feathers covering only strategic spots. A stocky man wearing an ill fitting tux was standing close, his arm dropped proprietarily over her shoulder. "And…. Santucci!"

"It looks like they really were a couple at one time. Let's get searching. I'm not sure the police are done with this place, so they could be back anytime."

"Good point. Don't think they'd much appreciate our helpfulness."

The search didn't take long. Although furniture cluttered the rooms, there were few drawers to hold much of anything. A thorough search of the small desk in the bedroom where they had entered produced nothing of interest.

"If anything of importance was kept here, it's gone now." Cece flipped through a few loose papers and grocery store sales slips from the main drawer. She pulled up a crumbled envelope already torn open. Empty. She glanced at the address on the front. To Dahlia Walker and a return address also in Phoenix. She dropped it back in with the rubble of broken pencils, old coupons, and paper clips—all the usual detritus of a typical junk drawer. She found nothing that spoke to anything but the ordinariness of life.

"Do you think the police have already finished with the house?" Heidi asked, as she looked through the two bedside tables.

"Probably. But like I said, if there was anything here, they've already gotten it. Remember that EMT told Maddie there was a suicide note. Just 'sorry.' Of course they would have taken that." Cece paused for a moment, uncertain. "So they're probably pretty sure it's a suicide. They'd still have to search but not so carefully. Just perfunctorily."

Cece stilled at a thought. "Can you murder someone and then string them up so it looks like they offed themselves?"

"In the crime shows I think you can. You can do most anything. But whether or not real people can do that, I don't know." Heidi was now rifling through the hangers of a cramped clothes closet. "Not so promising, " she sighed, shaking her head in disappointment. "She still has a closet full of costumes, feather boas and fancy hats. I wonder who she puts this stuff on for."

"Who knows what people do in private. Polyamory for the senior set? Don't want to know, for that matter."

"Much as I'd like to raid her stash of sexy costumes, I think we should we go." Cece glanced at her watch—10:32. "We're pushing our luck, I'm afraid. Let's make a cursory look at the rest and get out of here."

They skimmed through a small second bedroom and a narrow hall bathroom with a shower so tiny it couldn't be used if you weighed more than two hundred pounds. The narrow L-shaped living room-dining room combo had produced nothing.

They entered a small galley kitchen. Heidi started rifling through the drawers. "Nothing much here." Old mismatched flatware, used tin foil and plastic container lids. Two glasses sat in an otherwise empty sink. "At least she didn't hoard balls of string and stuff like that! You should have seen my grandma's kitchen back in Greenville, Texas. She had enough stuff to stock Goodwill for a year."

Cece laughed. "I had an uncle like that." She opened the pantry door and scanned the shelves. "Wait a sec. Look at those old canisters. A set. Very vintage. I bet an antique shop would want them. Just right for a retro kitchen redo." Heidi came over and peered over her shoulder.

"Pretty cool," she agreed.

Cece pulled the biggest one of the canisters off the shelf and set it on the counter. The red paint was faded, but flaked ornate deco-style lettering still clearly spelled out "FLOUR" in all caps.

Heidi looked at Cece. "Well, open it will you!"

She pulled off the lid and they both peered inside. Half full of flour. "I guess that's no surprise. No crown jewels!" Heidi shrugged in disappointment.

Cece was about to place the lid back when she hesitated. "My grandma had canisters like this. She told me once that that was where she stashed her "emergency" money. You have to put it where the boys don't look—or any of the men. She said she couldn't even have a bank account in her own name. And that was the fifties I think. If you ever needed to get money fast—like you had to escape or your husband disappeared or dropped dead or tried to murder you—you were on your own, you couldn't get into the bank account. Thus, the money stash!"

"Wow! That's pretty depressing. Anyway nothing there. So let's go."

Just to be sure, Cece poked her finger in and slowly circled through the flour. "Whoa Nelly, as grandma would say. I feel something!"

The tip of what looked like paper poked out from the flour

crater Cece had made. She pulled out a small torn piece of newspaper, folded and covered in flour. "What have we here?" She blew off the flour and unfolded the newspaper scrap pressing it open so it lay flat on the counter.

"It looks like an announcement, a baby announcement." She read, eyeing a faded photo of a newborn baby. "Baby Welsh, female, eight pounds six ounces, born at 4:46 p.m. April second at Phoenix General Hospital, Maricopa County, Arizona. It looks like a public record type announcement, not the kind the proud parents post."

"Is there a date for the paper?" Heidi asked.

Cece smoothed out the tip of the scrap, showing a part of the upper corner of the page.
"Just 985 is all there is. The rest is torn away."

"What is that? 985. Oh, of course. 1985. That's the date of the paper. A baby born April 2, 1985."

"Huh. That's a coincidence. Whoever that is turned—let me see—," Cece calculated in her head, "40, just yesterday! The day Dahlia died."

They looked at each other silently, eyes wide.

Just then the screech of a car nearby snapped them into the present.

"Take it and let's get out of here." Cece recovered the canister and shoved it back on the pantry shelf.

"Should we go back out the window?" Heidi turned toward the bedroom where they had come in.

"No, the back door. It's faster."

As they climbed quickly into Heidi's car, parked sufficiently far from the house, Heidi commented. "I guess Dahlia's not big on baking. Do you think she could have kept flour for 40 years?"

"Probably not. I bet that canister set belonged to her mother. Dahlia would have only been a teenager. I bet her mother hid it. Dahlia may have never known it was even there."
"Still, you'd think the cops would have searched the kitchen and found it."

"Guess not. Didn't talk to their grandmas enough!"

CHAPTER FIFTEEN

The B and B book club ladies convened that evening at Maddie's at seven, the regular book club hour. All were there except Stacey whose husband, Josh, was late coming home, so she had to stay with Ollie B until he got there. They waited chatting but avoiding the big topic until she could join them.

Not long after they were seated and enjoying refreshments, Stacey came into the living room breathlessly. "Ollie B demanded I come on time. According to her, she doesn't *need* a babysitter. Ha, no way I'm doing that, what with murderers, marauding teens, homeless crazy people and a wild ravaging tiger on the loose."

"Tut, tut," Anne intervened. "Crazy people experiencing not having a house, if you will. Plus it's not a tiger, for heaven's sake!"

"Sorry, Anne." She plopped down on the sofa, wiggling between Anne and Stephanie.

"What have I missed?" She looked expectantly at the ladies.

"You're good. We're just getting started."

More drinks were poured, the snacks shuffled onto plates and everyone looked to Maddie. "Well?"

"Getting information, I'm sorry to say, is getting a little harder now that this new death has happened. So of course the talk is that Dahlia hung herself knowing that the cops were closing in on her. She might have found out about Ryan's video. Not sure about that. Anyway I think she knew they were coming for her. If she was guilty, she probably thought it was hopeless and she'd go to prison. She's pretty old but not *that* old. A miserable future for sure. So I think most people involved in the case think she's guilty and her desperate act proves it."

"What about the suicide note?" That was the question they were all asking.

"The talk is that it was on paper from her desk and just one word, sorry, printed in all caps. I don't think there's much chance any expert could say for sure if it's her handwriting or not. But maybe. That is if there's doubt about the cause of death."

"And is there?" Cece looked around at the others for agreement.

Maddie shrugged. "Not clear. Maybe it's too soon to know but in a case like this the cops will have to make up their minds whether to pursue it or not pretty soon. They don't like to spend time on cases that they don't think will result in a conviction."

"Alright. So on to the next bit of news. Or at least Heidi and I think so." With that Cece described their adventure of the morning, with Heidi breaking in to add details.

"You guys are nuts!" Stephanie exclaimed. "We're going to have to bail you out of jail if you keep this up."

"Ha, ha! But the important thing is we found something interesting that we think needs to be further explored." Cece produced the folded newspaper scrap from her jacket pocket. After she read it out loud, a lengthy silence followed.

"So a baby. The notice hidden away where men would fail to ever find it. How old would Dahlia have been in 1985?" She looked around, eyebrows raised.

"OK, if Dahlia's in her fifties let's say, then she would have been born around 1969 or '70. So in 1985 she would have been......." Fingers counting. "...fifteen?"

"Maybe Dahlia's older. Then she'd have been seventeen or eighteen."

"So you all think this baby Welsh is Dahlia's baby?"

"Why not? None of us really know much about Dahlia and her life. Just that she's a loud dresser who was mad as hell at Santucci."

Cece sat quietly for a moment and then added, "At Santucci's funeral Dahlia claimed she'd had a relationship with him since she was fifteen. So that certainly suggests a baby, maybe a Santucci baby! Everybody thinks Dahlia worked as a stripper for Santucci in Vegas when he started out. I'm not sure she ever said that explicitly. So what if baby Welsh is Santucci's baby? Everybody thinks Dahlia hated Santucci because he tore down her mother's house and dumped her as well. What if there's more?"

Startled into silence by these new considerations, the group all sank back in their seats, contemplating the possibilities.

"We've got the date, the hospital, the city and the surname. How hard could it be to find out just who this baby is?" Stephanie nodded, looking around for confirmation.

"Not very!" They pretty much responded at once.

"Who wants to do it?" Cece asked, raised eyebrows. "Anne, haven't you done a lot of family history research?"

"I have and I will." Anne declared emphatically. "I'll find out just who baby Welsh is. I'll let you all know soon as I get it.

Maybe just a few days, depending on my work obligations."

"Good," Maddie joined in. "The coroner's report is due out soon. I don't think the medical examiner will be the one to do the death certification. Always depends on the backlog in a city as big as Phoenix. A cause of death has to be entered but that can be a tricky issue. Some coroners are more thorough than others. But what people are suspecting is that Dahlia's death will be ruled a suicide. Since she was the only known suspect in Santucci's death, his death can be ruled an accident, and since hers is a suicide, both cases can be closed with no one making a fuss about it. Sort of a win-win for the police department. Two successfully solved cases."

Stephanie chimed in, shaking her head emphatically. "But what about our new evidence? A possible third party who could impact what happened at least to Dahlia and maybe Santucci as well."

"Let's not get ahead of ourselves. We need solid facts. Who is baby Welsh and is there any reason to think she's involved in any way? Until we know that we can't make any assumptions. Remember in 1985 DNA testing did not exist. And now it's ubiquitous. So we'll probably be able to track the baby's mother if not the father."

"What about Dahlia?" Cece reached for another brownie and slowly bit off a corner. "We really don't know much about her for sure, do we?" She looked at the others.

Pretty much blank faces all around.

"We need to get her history. There's all the gossip about her working as a stripper for Santucci. And her claiming to be his fiancee until he stole her mother's house out from under her and then sent her packing. At least that's the story and she says pretty much the same thing. Everyone knows she hates him and can't let the past go. And then the story she told at his funeral. Where did that come from? So why can't she move on?"

"We need to know the whole story, that's for sure," Anne added.

"I hate to bring this up, Cece and Heidi, but what about the newspaper clipping? Isn't it evidence? It came from a cordoned off potential crime scene so shouldn't it be turned over to the police?"

"Ekkk! Bite your tongue." Cece exclaimed. "How would we explain having it? Don't think we could say we just happened to drop by the death house and picked it up. Anyway it isn't a "crime" scene if Dahlia committed suicide. Offing yourself isn't a crime, is it?"

"Maybe a sin, some think, but not a crime." They nodded agreement.

"Hold on, ladies." Stephanie held out both hands, palms up. "We're not going to get ourselves—we're all accomplices to whatever any of us do—into trouble. We're helping because we know the police, poor dears, are so overworked. And we definitely know what happens to cases they don't want to prosecute—right?—cases closed. Just ask the parents in Gilbert!"

Cece leaned forward in her chair. "Plus the police have no way of knowing where this came from." She reached for the clipping and held it up. "They should have searched more thoroughly, but they didn't. So we're investigating because clearly they didn't. I think they just want this whole thing to go away."

Stacey added, "And they don't even care about the ocelot and how it got loose. Or where it is."

Right, they agreed. Heartless. "And think of our little doggies. They're not cat food."

CHAPTER SIXTEEN

As promised, Anne texted the book clubbers only four days later. "I've got news," she announced. "As in *bingo!!*"

When all the ladies had arrived, opened the bottles and cans they brought, poured their drinks and shared their various contributions to the snack table, Anne began.

"I went to public records to find baby Welsh. Not hard. She was born to Dahlia Welsh in Phoenix, Arizona in 1985. Dahlia! That we were already pretty sure of. No father is listed. Her name on her birth certificate is Hope Welsh. After that there are no more entries for a Hope Welsh born in Phoenix, Arizona. She's off the radar which suggests she probably was put up for adoption and the records were sealed which, I think, was not unusual at the time."

A mummer of disappointment traveled around the living room.

"What about Dahlia? What did you find about her." Heidi broke the silence. "She's the key to all of this."

"Right you are." Anne nodded curtly, popping some Trader Joe's popcorn into her mouth. "So, that's next. Here's the record that I could find through the website Truth Finders."

"You have to pay for that," Stacey interrupted.

"No worries," Anne continued. "Not that expensive. You just have to remember to cancel your account once you've got what you want. Anyway, Dahlia was born Dahlia Welsh in 1970 to Amanda Welsh. Again no father listed. She attended Prescott High School in Prescott, Arizona in 1984, her freshman year, but apparently then dropped out after that first year."

"That was before the arrival of baby Welsh," Cece murmured.

"Yes, so the next entry is the birth of baby Welsh in Phoenix."

"So she leaves Prescott. Maybe she got sent away because she was pregnant. Like a home for unwed mothers."

"Were those still around?" Cece asked.

"Not sure," Anne continued. "Maybe she ran away. Abusive boyfriend."

"Or mother's boyfriend." Ideas were floating around abundantly.

"Next known address is in Las Vegas, Nevada. So, yes. Bingo. That's obviously where she met up with Santucci. I haven't traced Santucci's record yet, after he left West High, but I can.

"Anyway, she has a number of addresses for the next few years, probably floating around in different rentals. No record of home ownership, one short-lived marriage in 1997 to an Alex Walker, divorce two years later, no more babies. Known employment—a number of casinos and clubs in Vegas and nearby towns. Including clubs owned by Santucci who by this time seems pretty well established in the gaming industry.

"In 2015, she shows up in Phoenix, listing an address at her mother's house on Palm Lane as her residence. Amanda Welsh is now in her seventies and Dahlia is 45. She lists herself as a caregiver.

Anne paused giving everyone time to mull this all over. "What a history," Cece said, frowning into her wine glass. "Must have been a hard life. If I'd known all this I might have liked her a little better. Or at least been more tolerant. Maybe she was a victim of sexual abuse. Pregnant at fifteen and that's it. She's gone. It must have been awful."

"Right." General agreement and head nods.

"That's almost all," Anne continued. "I found her mother's death record. She died of lung cancer in 2018. Dahlia was apparently her only child and so inherited her mother's house on Palm Lane.

"The next record of the Palm Lane house after Dahlia got it shows ownership transferring to Sal Santucci through a quit claim deed recorded in 2020."

"So that's it, ladies. What do you all think?"

There was quiet for a few minutes before Heidi broke into the silence. "I've seen the records for the Santucci property in Encanto. It wasn't long after that that he acquired a building permit for his house, allowing him to demolish the house next to Dahlia's as well as Dahlia's. He somehow got a special variance to tear down the houses. The neighborhood became recognized as historic in the 1980's, so after that, all demolition and building has to be approved by the historic preservation department at city planning and zoning."

"How on earth did he get that monstrosity of a house approved in a historic neighborhood?" Cece blurted out.

"Right," Heidi continued. "That's exactly what everybody was asking. It's possible that he submitted a different set of plans but then built what he wanted. There was talk that the regular inspector had taken a leave of absence and was replaced by a temp. But by the time it was obvious that what he was building had no place in an historic neighborhood, it was too late. He had done it. And to make it worse, he always bragged about it, how he could control everything, everybody, and do exactly what he wanted."

"No surprise he's dead. Just desserts, I say." Stephanie snorted before taking a big breath and continuing, "But he's not married, right, and has no known children, right?"

Since none of them had the slightest idea, they shook their heads. "I've been in the neighborhood the longest," Anne said. "Of course Santucci went to high school here but left and didn't come back to this neck of the woods until he bought the Scottsdale club, got involved with Dahlia and her mother's house, and started the whole building process. But there's never been any mention of ex-wives or children or anything else. That doesn't mean they aren't out there. So let's see if anyone comes out of the proverbial woodwork!"

"A guy like Santucci," Cece added. "I bet he's got a few unacknowledged kids scattered around."

"There're far too many kids with no fathers around…and thanks to our beautiful Supreme Court's new ruling, we're going to have a lot more in the near future." Stephanie sighed, with a deep scowl.

"Ladies, whoa now, the real question is, "who is baby Welsh?" What happened to her? Are there ways to trace adoptions?"

They all looked nonplussed, head shaking all around.

"Maybe," Anne ventured. "I think a lot has changed with the advent of DNA testing. "I'll look into it."

Heidi bolted upright in her chair. "Wait." She held up her slender arm, waving them to her. She turned to Cece. "Listen up. Cece, remember when we were at Dahlia's house Tuesday? I was going through the desk. I vaguely remember an envelope in the top drawer. I saw it was torn open and the letter was gone so I went on and didn't give it any thought. It was addressed to Dahlia, Dahlia Walker, I think. I just glanced at the return address in the corner. I think I mentioned it. I'm pretty sure it was a Phoenix address and I remember thinking that it was odd for someone in town to write a letter to someone else in town. Like no one does that any more, right? So I just forgot about it."

"Maybe it was a thank you note. Some people still write those."

"You're right. I write them to potential clients, people I want to remember me and how nice and professional I am."

"Ha, ha, Heidi. You don't have to write any thank you notes for people to know how sweet you are!" Cece exclaimed.

Heidi blew her an air kiss. "Thanks, dear one!"

"Back to topic," Cece continued. "So, Heidi, are you thinking it's worth getting that envelope and checking it out. That maybe it's someone important to all this mess?"

Heidi shook her head, her bobbed hair bouncing about her cheeks. "Don't know. It's a long shot."

"A wild goose chase," Stephanie added, glancing out the front window of Anne's living room. Darkness not yet descending. "But if the death was filed as suicide, the house might not be cordoned off any more."

"And that means, it'll be cleaned out to put back on the rental market," Heidi added. "Probably soon. Landlords don't like their rental properties sitting empty. No cash flow. Not to mention its proximity to downtown and the horde of vagrants roaming around."

Cece looked around. "So what are we waiting for. Let's go."

"What! Now??" They chorused.

Cece was already picking up her purse. "Why not? It's only a few minutes away. Heidi and I already know how to get in. We could zip in there in a few minutes, grab the envelope and be out of there in a cat's whisker. If we wait until tomorrow it could be too late. It might already be too late."

"Cat's whisker??"

"You know what I mean. Who's in?" She scanned the others. They all stared at her, eye brows arched, faces scrunched.

Heidi sighed, "I'm in." Nods all around.

Anne muttered as they started gathering their things, "Exactly why are we doing this? It's not like it's any of our business. We don't have any skin in the game."

Cece paused. She turned to Anne and gently squeezed her arm. "I know what you're feeling. It's true enough that it isn't really any of our business. Maybe it's because she's there. A person, she's there and then she isn't. It's strange, like it's so anonymous. She's anonymous. And then to die with so many questions unanswered. It's deeply unsettling."

"I wouldn't call Dahlia anonymous exactly, someone so "put it all out there."

"Yeah, but the real person. We just saw her stereotype. An old stripper desperately marketing her 'put it all out there'. A slab of meat on the butcher block of male lust. The kind that hold back all women by reinforcing the idea that only highly sexualized women are worth a man's notice."

"A slab of meat on the butcher block of male lust? I like that. May I quote you," Stephanie chimed in.

"Ha, ha. I think someone else probably said that. But anyway it works."

"She's just there. That's why we care."

"That sounds like a Hallmark card—or the climber, Sir Edmund Hillary, when he was asked why he wanted to climb Mount Everest. He said, "because it's there.""

"Works for me." Stacey stood abruptly. "Let's roll.""

CHAPTER SEVENTEEN

Dark had settled over the Story neighborhood as the two cars turned onto Pierce Street. They proceeded according to plan. Anne, Stacey, and Stephanie stayed in one car that they parked across the street from Dahlia's house. They were to keep watch over the house to make sure no one was around and there was no danger. Their cell phones were out, ready to instantly warn Cece and Heidi if anything happened that could be in any way threatening.

"If I'd known we were going to do a stakeout tonight," Stephanie grumbled, "I'd have worn all black."

"We'll all scrunch down," Stacey countered. They slumped lower in their seats and turned to watch the darkened small house. "It looks sad," she added wistfully. "All dark and lonely. Like the story it told had dragged it down."

Cece and Heidi continued on to the end of the street and parked out of sight of the house. They slipped out of the car after making sure the street was empty. In only a few minutes they reached the side yard of Dahlia's house and edged through the gate, still unlocked, to the back of the house.

Cece went directly to the window they had so recently pried

open. It was now closed.

"Hope they didn't latch it from the inside," she said, prying her fingernails under the steel window frame.

"Thank goodness, no one latched it," Heidi breathed. She turned to look at Cece. "Guess that's me again." She sighed. "Gimme a hand."

Repeating their process of a few days ago, Heidi wiggled through the window and dropped onto the bed still pushed against the wall. Quickly she jumped off the bed and headed for the back door to let Cece in.

"Looks like no one else has been here," Cece remarked as she surveyed the living room and dining area. "A furnished rental. Good for us."

They went into the small bedroom to the desk tucked into the corner of the room. Hardly enough room for a desk chair. Hurriedly Cece pulled open the top drawer. It was gone!

"Quick, Heidi. Shine your cell phone light in here. It's too dark."

Heidi stood behind Cece shining the light into the drawer. "There it is." She flashed the beam into the back corner of the drawer. A white crumpled up envelope was smooched into the back slat of the drawer.

Cece reached in. "Got it. Let's go."

Just then her cell phone rang, making them both jump at the sudden loud noise.

"Get out. Someone's outside standing on the front walk, looking at the house. **Get out! They're going toward the door!"**

Cece stuffed the envelope into her pocket and they ran for the back door banging into the dining area chairs in the process. They flung the door open.

"Shhh. Behind me," Cece's arm jutted out to block Heidi. They crouched down. Heidi held on to the back of Cece's jacket as they crept single file out the door and over to the overgrown driveway leading to the garage. "Follow me," Cece whispered as she pulled Heidi toward a row of bedraggled oleanders that marked the property line with the next yard.

Seeing a break in the bushes, Cece held back branches, letting Heidi through and into the neighboring yard. They crossed it close against the thankfully darkened house, and quickly reached the far side of the yard. Sounds of canned laughter drifted out from the back of the house.

"Glad the porch light isn't on," Cece breathed.

They stopped and turned to look back at the front sidewalk of Dahlia's house. No one was in sight but thick bushes obscured the view of all but the yard closest to the sidewalk. Cece pulled out her cell.

"Is it safe now?" she whispered into the phone.

"I think so. Did you get it? Where are you anyway?" Stacey hammered out the questions.

"Yeah, we got it. Now we're at the far side of the yard just east of the house."

"Good, good. Whoever's there just turned toward the gate on the west side where you guys got in. Wait a sec."

Cece and Heidi stood rigid, waiting, barely breathing.

"Ok, he's through the gate and going toward the backyard. Can't see him anymore. Cross the street quickly and walk back to your car on this side of the street. Make it fast—no, no, don't make it fast. Act natural. Oh, I don't know. Just get out of there. We're driving up to where your car is. We'll watch just to make sure you're safe." She started the engine and slowly pulled out from the curb just as Cece and Heidi scurried across the street to the far sidewalk.

Stacey idled at the side of the street as Cece and Heidi flung open the doors and jumped into their car. She looked over and buzzed her window down. "Back to my house? Yes?"

Within ten minutes they were back in Anne's living room, breathlessly devouring the last of the snacks and generally milling around, winding down from the excitement of the past half hour.

"Nothing like a little adventure to bring on an appetite!" Cece moaned, downing another tortilla chip with a scoop of bean dip.

"That all happened pretty fast," Stacey exclaimed.

"Told you." Heidi said.

"I've got it!" Cece reached into her jacket pocket and pulled out the crumpled envelope. "Voila! Let's hope it actually has some meaning." She held it up for everyone to see. With a dramatic flourish she spread it open against her jean clad thigh and read.

"Morgan Thompson, 965 W. Roosevelt Ave. Phoenix, Arizona.   And the postmark. March 8th."

"So what now? How do we find out about Morgan Thompson?"

"Yeah, Morgan, male or female? Probably female. That was a popular name a while back."

They all nodded.

"We're not going there tonight. That's for sure." Anne shook her head. "I'll see what I can find out online and I'll let you know. Public records, Facebook account, Instagram, whatever. I'll text you all whether it's wasted time or maybe something interesting."

"That's a plan. I gotta get home. George is a worrier and so far he's not been too bothered by all this sleuthing. But I don't want to push it."

They all agreed. A waste of time, most likely. Or not.

CHAPTER EIGHTEEN

"She grew up in Prescott," Anne announced once the B and B ladies had settled in three days later.

"Oh my gosh! That's where Dahlia lived!" Stephanie said, waving her wine glass around enough to slosh out a splatter of merlot. "Whoops, sorry."

"Right, and her birth date—April 2, 1985! So, bingo again. We found her! Morgan Thompson is Baby Welsh! As you can see, ladies, we figured it out." She smiled broadly around the room. "But to go on. She graduated with an associates from Yavapai Community College in 2005 and started at ASU the following fall. She graduated with a B.A. in Music in 2008."

"So Dahlia clearly is her mother. But did she know her? Why would Morgan Thompson write a letter to Dahlia? If they knew about each other and had a relationship, she wouldn't write a letter. That seems very formal. She would call or text, not write a letter." Cece chewed on a gluten-free brownie, thoughtfully, wiping the crumbs back onto her snack plate.

"Hold on. Maybe she would write a letter. We know Dahlia is her birth mother. We know Morgan is the daughter that was adopted by someone else. If it's her first contact with her biological mother, doesn't it make sense that she would send a letter rather than something more personal. You hear stories about people who find parents, children, siblings or whatever and when they meet up the first time, if they do, it doesn't always go well. It's very risky. Better to send a letter and see if or how she responds."

Everyone perked up and leaned forward toward Anne, as expectant as if she were about to bestow the Nobel Prize of Literature.

"She's a musician," Anne continued. "She lives in the Roosevelt Arts District and has her own band. She writes her own music and plays gigs in a lot of different places, public and private. I heard her play on her Instagram account and she's really good. At least I think so.

"Anyway, there're a lot of postings of her and her live-in boyfriend, a cute mutt dog and maybe some other friends who go in and out. It looks like a pretty noveau-hippy vibe. She advertises where the band plays."

"Cool. Maybe she's happy." Stephanie nodded approvingly.

"I listened to one of her songs," Anne continued. "It was sweet, wistful. About someone lost and maybe found again. A hopeful longing made more so by a heart wrenching melody."

"A lost mother, maybe?" Cece whispered.

"A found mother, maybe?" Stacey added.

"A dead mother! Let's remember that. So what did Morgan know? We need to find out or we'll never understand the whole story." Heidi looked around at her friends.

"Perfect." Cece clapped her hands. "Field trip!"

"Friday night. It just so happens she's playing at the Egyptian on Grand Avenue."

"Yayyy! I've been wanting to go there."

"Me too."

"Should we go for dinner. That Mexican restaurant inside the Egyptian is supposed to be great."

"I'll make the reservations. Husbands??"

"Sure, why not?"

"Because it will be harder to meet with her and try to pry out information if we have a bunch of impatient guys around wanting to go home to watch the Suns or whatever."

"Ok. I have an idea." Cece got everyone's attention and went on. "Let's just go with husbands but try to see her on our own. Leave the guys at the table and go backstage to see if we can meet her. Maybe try to strike up a conversation during a break. Something like that. Play it by ear. Then we can decide the next step. After all, we know who she is but how much does she know? And if she does know who her mother is, does she also know that she is now dead and what all does that mean?"

"You're right. There's a lot going on and we have no idea about any of it. We need to proceed slowly and decide how to go forward once we know more." Stephanie, always the voice of reason.

"Maybe she murdered her mother, revenge for rejecting her as a baby," Stacey added.

Cece punched her arm. "You're awful, Stacey. What child would murder her own mother?"

Stacey looked at Heidi and they both laughed, "Mine!" they chorused.

Friday afternoon came soon enough. George was blowing his nose and being very grumpy when Cece reminded him of their reservation at the Egyptian.

"I don't feel like it. I feel sick, maybe Covid. Probably Covid. Why would I want to go hear loud music in a crowded restaurant with no doubt overpriced food when I'm sick?"

"It's tacos for heaven's sake. But the music is outside. Very casual. It'll be fun. Come on. We haven't been out for a while. You'll love it!"

"Ha! No, I won't. You go. You'll have fun. Live it up. I'm very happy to stay home and watch the game. Besides, I really don't feel well. I'm probably contagious. And it's cold out!"

Cece cocked an eye at him appraisingly. "Hummm." She placed a hand on his forehead. "You feel all right to me. But okay. Stay home and miss the fun."

"Thank you, thank you." George wiped a dramatic hand across his face. He brightened. "You could bring me a *churro*." Eyebrows raised, sweet smile.

Cece laughed, "Oh, okay, sick boy."

⟡

The Egyptian Motor Hotel had been a run-down fifties motel on Grand Avenue in the days when it was the road to Vegas and not much else. Years had not been kind and the neighborhood had become blighted by drugs, vagrants and crime. So the restoration of the motel with a retro vib had been a boost to the neighborhood that was struggling to become a bona fide arts district.

They all settled into the Adirondack style chairs that were scattered around the lawn in front of a raised platform stage and ordered tacos and drinks from the takeout window of the restaurant attached to the motel. The band played a variety of music and the evening passed enjoyably enough for everyone.

At the break Heidi and Cece decided they would be the ones to try to get a word with Morgan. All of them might be too much. They were definitely trying to stay low key.

Heidi led the way because she had been there once before and remembered the layout.

They had easily identified Morgan. Her dark curly hair framed a wide face with friendly eyes and an engaging smile. She was drinking a beer with one of the band members behind the stage in the swimming pool area. They were sitting on the steps of a sleek airstream trailer that added to the fifties motif of the motel.

"Hey, we love your music," Cece blurted out, smiling broadly.

"Your singing is so full of heart. It's beautiful," Heidi added.

"Well thank you, ladies. I'm glad you enjoyed it. I have wonderful band members. They make everything sound good." She smiled, pushing a stray curl behind her ear and turning to the bearded man standing at her side. "This is Vincent, my partner. And I'm Morgan. But I guess you know that."

"Partner and more," he smiled wrapping an arm across her shoulders.

"Yes, true," she laughed at him. Turning back, she asked, "Is this your first time here?"

"I've been here once before, right after the opening. I love this place," Heidi added, waving an arm toward the stage.

"Yeah. It's a great place. Good that the building was restored rather than torn down. Anyway, we've got to get back. So glad you all are having a good time." With that they put down their drinks, gathered up the instruments and returned to the stage.

"Did you find her?" The ladies asked in a rush when Cece and Heidi got back to their table.

"Did you meet her?" The questions were flying.

"Just for a few minutes backstage. Also met the boyfriend but it was brief. But they both seemed nice, so that's all good." Heidi stopped long enough to spot Vincent just sitting back down at the grand piano. "There," she pointed.

"Humm. Cute! But Morgan?"

"She just chatted with us briefly. But she was sweet. She has such a kind voice, if voices can be kind anyway," Cece said. "I think I like her."

"Me too," Heidi chimed in.

"Mission accomplished?" Hector, Heidi's husband, asked.

"Yes, for now."

CHAPTER NINETEEN

The next Tuesday the neighborhood board meeting convened at seven as usual. It had been moved from its usual spot to accommodate the home tour and all the work that went into making that a success. Part of this night's agenda was an assessment of the tour. The success of the tour affected the success of the garden club and all structures within the neighborhood.

Brett Riley, the neighborhood board president, started the meeting. Monthly board meetings were also held in the garden clubhouse which sat on the corner of Fifteenth Avenue and Coronado Road. Besides neighborhood meetings it hosted any number of events both neighborhood based or citywide. Weddings, religious meetings, art shows, bonsai sales and whatever brought an income to sustain the building and its gardens.

Heidi and Stacey were garden club members as well as board members and they were in their chairs pulled up to the u-shaped tables that seated all the members. Cece was sitting in the audience, small as it was. She was there for a reason. She knew that Stanley Mortimer was giving a presentation on his prize irises and she was very much interested. It was unusual to have a presentation outside of the usual board business but the iris club had been suspended for a number of months due to the illness of its president. Some of the neighbors were anxious to see Stanley's irises because he sold the tubers to anyone in the neighborhood who wanted them. Since this was the time of year that the irises had to be purchased, the presentation could not be delayed. And Cece definitely wanted some.

Brett soon introduced Joyce, the chair of the home tour committee. She began, "As you all no doubt know, the last few weeks have been a bigger surprise than any of us could have imaged. To have a murder on our home tour is something that has never happened before. On all our tours over almost fifty years we've never had so much as a serious accident, even with literally tens of thousands of people touring our homes over that time. We knew of the death only minutes after the start of the tour and a huge number of tickets had already been sold. I had to immediately announce that house number nine was no longer on the tour due to unfortunate unforeseen circumstances. Somehow the word got out that the owner was found dead in his yard. 'Dead' morphed into 'murdered' almost instantaneously and a huge ruckus ensued. And—we immediately sold out the rest of the tickets!" Joyce shrugged her shoulders and spread her arms in the universal 'who could predict' fashion.

"So, thanks to morbid curiosity, this home tour was the biggest success ever."

A few of the board members broke out clapping but suddenly stopped, embarrassed by their enthusiasm. Applauding a murder was a bit *gauche*. Not quite appropriate under the circumstances!

"What's the status of the investigation? Is it a murder for

sure?" Someone piped up from the small audience. The board members all looked at Joyce, as if she had the answer to the final Wheel Of Fortune spin. She quickly turned the meeting back to Brett.

"I contacted the police department and their answer was that the cause of death had been ruled undetermined. The case has been closed for lack of evidence. After the suicide of Dahlia Walker, no further evidence had been obtained so there was at least for now nothing to investigate. The detective said it was always possible if more evidence was found that the case could be reopened. But for now, it's closed."

A murmur went around the room. Then silence fell as each considered the very unsatisfactory outcome of all the chaos that had consumed the neighborhood since March sixteenth. People want answers, definites, not maybes. Human nature rebels against ambiguity, Cece thought. She shifted in her chair, impatient to keep the agenda moving along so she could see the iris presentation that she had come for.

"And what about the homeless camp? No one is doing anything and it's getting bigger and bigger every day." An angry voice half shouted from the back row of the audience section. "What's the good of clearing out the Zone if they just move into other neighborhoods. And now they're here!" he added, his fist punching the air above his head as if to ward off those lurking imaginary adversaries.

That generated some head nods and mumbled agreement.

"We've contacted the police, and the organization Phoenix Cares," Brett responded, "and they're working on it. They say it will be cleared out soon." That brought on more complaints but finally the meeting moved on, returning to the list of agenda topics.

But to Cece, the meeting, like most meetings, seemed to drone on forever, going over the particulars of the tour and the other board sponsored activities in the neighborhood until finally the iris presentation started. The lights were darkened to better see the vivid colors on the screen, as Stanley Mortimer set up his computer and power point to start his talk.

Cece could tell Stanley was a socially awkward man. He was tall and lanky but his clothes were ill fitting, hanging off his body like an old bathrobe on the closet hook. His thinning hair was turning to grey. He wore round wire-rimmed glasses that magnified his pale blue eyes—large eyes that seemed somewhat predatory above a prominent beak-like nose. All together he looked like some kind of large raptor watching for an unsuspecting mouse. His speech at the beginning paused, uncomfortably too often, but as he talked and gazed at the photographs of his stunning beaded iris, he grew more confident until he was almost floating with his delight in his creations.

"This is my finest," he said, smiling for the first time as he aimed a thin pointer at screen. "The Lady Lorraine! I've worked so hard for the last few years to find a way to honor my late wife. And this finally is it."

Stanley did not elaborate on the details of the circumstances that surrounded the death of his wife but everyone in the neighborhood knew. He had received many consoling notes from the board and from many neighbors when they found out what had happened. Shortly after Stanley retired from his years at Intel, his wife was called to her mother's bedside in San Diego. Lorraine Mortimer left Palmcroft in the spring of 2022 when the Covid epidemic was growing. Her elderly mother in California had unfortunately contracted a severe case and Lorraine went to be by her side and nurse her back to health. But things had turned out differently. Lorraine's mother died of Covid complications and Lorraine came down with the illness too. She was too sick to travel back to Phoenix so Stanley decided to be with her in California. By the time he realized how seriously ill she was, it was too late. She died before he made it to her mother's home.

Cece had never seen such a dejected man when he returned to Palmcroft. He became almost totally isolated, spending all his time developing his iris specimens. He was only now gradually coming back into the world and Cece was glad to see it. Life was for the living after all. She had seen way too much death in the last two months and she was glad to see poor Stanley coming out of his shell. She tore her eyes from the screen to Stanley's smiling face. Hmmmm. A barn owl, perhaps.

She switched her focus back to the screen, watching in rapt attention as the photograph of the gorgeous Lady Lorraine virtually radiated off the screen. Rosy-peach top petals furling upward from a sky blue bearded base. Magnificent! It was as if a bluebird had transformed into a flower. She must have some!

Stanley ended his presentation with an invitation to those present to stop by his garden and select the irises of their choice. They could be paid for, tagged and in several months after the blooms had died back, they could be delivered for transplantation into their new gardens.

When the meeting was finally over, Cece gathered her things, said goodbye to her fellow B and B buddies and walked toward the door. As she opened the door to the parking lot, she ran into Stanley, loaded up with his presentation gear.

"Here, let me," she said, holding open the door so Stanley

could go through. "Your iris are magnificent. I'm definitely going to come by and pick some out."

"Don't wait too long." He muttered into his chest, readjusting his armload to keep his things from tumbling to the ground. A notebook slid off.

"I'm so sorry. Let me." Cece exclaimed, scrambling to pick it up and place it back on his things.

"Just c-c-clumsy me." Stanley had a slight stutter which Cece hadn't noticed during his talk. But once away from his presentation equipment and out into the world of human interaction, he seemed to shrink into himself, reverting back to a quiet unassuming discomfort. His inspired demeanor as a scientist and iris hybridizer had wilted, left behind at the podium. Bless his little heart, Cece thought with an inward chuckle, remembering their book club banter. She smiled a last time before turning toward her car in the parking lot.

CHAPTER TWENTY

Cece and Anne decided to go back to the Egyptian on Thursday for happy hour. It was the late afternoon hour when Morgan and Vincent played together without accompaniment from the band. Only their guitars. Their first song was a solo for Morgan, with Vincent accompanying her on guitar.

Cece and Anne settled into their chairs, margaritas in hand, to enjoy the beauty of the music. "She has a voice like Joan Collins," Anne whispered. Cece nodded agreement.

Morgan introduced her next song. "This one I have only recently written. It comes from a place deep in my heart. I hope you all enjoy it."

She started strumming the melody to a low humming introduction. But then the words! Anne and Cece were spellbound.

"It could have been, it should have been... that everything would change. They told me wrong but now I know. Now I know what could have been... How was I to know what they said was true."

The lyrics rolled sweetly over Cece with a pulsing rhythm,

slow and yearning. When the song ended, Morgan looked down at her guitar, fussing with the strings to cover a backhanded swipe at the glistening on her cheek.

When her set ended Morgan slung her guitar along her side and joined Vincent in disappearing into the back of the restaurant.

"Come on." Anne set down her drink and motioned to Cece to get up.

"It's going to be pretty embarrassing if we're wrong about all of this," Cece muttered.

"No, it won't," Anne protested. "We can find out in a minute if we're right. If we're wrong, we'll just compliment her beautiful song and come back here and finish our drinks and head for home."

"Right."

They caught up with Morgan in a back staging room. She was sitting with Vincent who was busily tuning his guitar.

"We saw you last week," Anne began hesitantly. "We love your music and wanted to hear more. We're wondering if you always play here. Are you local?"

Morgan smiled and nodded. "Yeah, I'm local for now."

"Did you grow up here?"

"No, Prescott. But I went to school here and of course Phoenix has a lot more opportunities for musicians than small towns like Prescott. So I just stayed."

Cece and Anne exchanged a quick glance at that news. Surely that meant they were right.

"Yeah," Vincent butted in. "And there's me." He grinned at the ladies.

"Yes." Morgan patted his knee. "There's you."

Taking a deep breath Anne said, "Your song is so wistful, so sad but you, I'm happy to say, seem very happy. I hope everything is all right."

Morgan hesitated. "Yes, I'm happy now but I've just recently had a bunch of happy and sad events that I had not expected."

"I'm sorry to hear that," Cece said.

A far away looked flicked across Morgan's eyes. "My mother," she said softly.

Cece glanced at Anne, who nodded her head slightly. "Dahlia Welsh." Her voice dropped to almost a whisper.

Morgan started and blinked at them, eyes wide with surprise. "What?? How do you know my mother?" she exclaimed with a look somewhere between horror and amazement. "Who are you?"

Vincent leaned over and took her hand. He, too, looked askance at Anne and Cece, waiting for an answer.

Cece started, "We live in Encanto-Palmcroft and we knew your mother. Not well," she added quickly. "But we know about Santucci's death and your mother's involvement with him."

Morgan bristled at that, shaking her head as if she would not accept the words.

"But we know more about your mother's death. And we're so sorry, so sorry for your loss. We, well Anne and I and three of our friends, have some ideas about what happened. We don't believe the police are going to do an investigation of your mother's death."

Morgan stared at them, wide eyed. "Why are you here? I don't understand. Are you detectives? Private investigators?" She was becoming more and more agitated.

"No, no," both Cece and Anne hastened to answer.

"Well, what then?" Morgan glanced at her watch. "We have to get back out. I can't talk about it now. Can we meet later?" She gaped at them, clearly confused and worried.

"Could we meet tomorrow morning at, eh, the First Watch coffee shop on Thomas Road? Do you know it? We would have more time to explain how we know about your mother and the circumstances surrounding her death."

"Yes, I know that place. I'll be there at nine," Morgan said, picking up her guitar and motioning Vincent to follow her back into the lounge area. She left so fast that Cece and Anne stood frozen until finally they looked at each other and shook their heads in mutual amazement.

"What do you think?" Cece asked once they were back in their car.

"Whew, hard to say. She's obviously upset but I don't know if it's aimed at us or all the other stuff that has happened. Hopefully we'll find out tomorrow."

CHAPTER TWENTY-ONE

Morgan was already sitting at a booth by the window at First Watch nursing a cup of coffee when Cece and Anne pushed open the doors. She looked up and watched them closely as they proceeded to her table. Suspicious, Cece thought. And no wonder. Their showing up out of the blue. But Cece was hoping that Morgan wanted to know more. Maybe anything that would help her to understand her past. Cece and Anne slid into the booth across from Morgan.

"I'm glad you've come," Anne started. "We were afraid that maybe this was just too weird for you. Our showing up and not really being able to explain very well why we wanted to know you."

At that moment a waitress came by with a coffee pot and cups. "Coffee?" She nodded toward Cece and Anne. "Refill?" to Morgan.

"Sure," all three said at virtually the same time. That brought a small laugh that lightened the moment.

When the waitress had left, Anne started to explain. She told Morgan how they had gotten involved in the home tour and how Cece had discovered Santucci's body in the fish pond. They also told Morgan as much as they could about Dahlia's relationship with Santucci and her anger at him. Obviously their catty criticism of the way Dahlia dressed and behaved was left behind. She didn't need to know that.

"The long and the short of it is that we don't think the police have done their job. We think they just saw an opportunity to close a case that they didn't want to deal with and made a decision to end the investigation. They say they'll reopen the case if more evidence shows up but we think that's b.s. We are not sure that your mother committed suicide. After we found out about your existence, we became even more convinced that your mother would want to live."

"But how do you know about our relationship? I only found out myself in the last month or so and as far as I know no one else knows. I haven't told anyone….so how do you know?" She arched her eyebrows, her eyes shifting from one to the other.

"That's a long story," Cece said, "but just briefly, we found a newspaper birth announcement with your name on it in your mother's things after she died. It wasn't your name now but your birth surname, Welsh. That was your mother's name as we're sure you know now."

"Yes, I do know that. But why did you have my mother's things?" Morgan's face wrinkled in confusion.

"That's another long story. We suspected that you had contacted her because we found a letter you sent to her. Well, not the letter but the envelope with the addresses and we put two and two together. But, of course, we don't know what happened between the two of you. We're only guessing. I can't tell you exactly why we have gotten involved but maybe it's because we're all mothers and it just seems like the two of you have a story."

Morgan had sat quietly stirring her coffee absently as Anne recounted all of this. She looked hard from one to the other, evaluating, judging. Did she want to talk to them? Snoopy bored ladies looking for vicarious excitement? She paused, a long breath seeping from her lips, before her face softened and a tear rimmed her eyelid.

"I didn't even know I was adopted," she started. "I only found out recently. Can you believe that? In this day, I thought everybody knew stuff like that. But my mother, well I guess now I have to say my adoptive mother, went into the hospital six months ago with breast cancer. She only lasted a few months before she was gone." She paused again fighting to keep back the tears.

Cece reached over and covered her hand with her own. "You have had too much tragedy," she said softly.

Morgan wiped away her tears with a napkin and continued, "My mother said she needed to tell me that I was adopted because I needed to know the medical history of my biological parents. Once she became so sick she knew that I had the right to know my own family history. To know more about my own health if for no other reason. She told me that she had wanted to tell me but had never seemed to find the right time. And then I left home for school and she just never did. But when she became so ill, she knew she had to tell me. She didn't even know who my biological parents were. They wanted a closed adoption so she knew nothing about them. I was adopted within the first month of my life so I never knew anything. Of course she knew about DNA testing and encouraged me to search for my biological parents. Then at least I would have a better idea of any genetic problems I might be susceptible to.

"At first I didn't want to know. It made me angry that I had

had a mother who didn't want me. What kind of mother doesn't want her own baby?"

Anne and Cece nodded, not knowing how to respond. How would they feel in her place? It was all very confusing.

"Anyway," Morgan continued. "Vincent talked me into changing my mind. He said I needed to know at least something about my biological heritage. That made sense and in reality I was curious. I wanted to know but was so afraid it would end badly and I'd be heartbroken. After all the only mother I'd even known was dead and she and my father had gotten a divorce when I was only in grade school. He was never much part of my life so when she died I was really feeling like an orphan. Pretty silly since I was almost forty."

"Not silly," Cece murmured.

"Reluctantly," Morgan continued, "I sent in a swab to 23and-Me several months ago. It took awhile to get the results but once I did it wasn't too hard to track down Dahlia. I found her mother who had her DNA on file because of her illness. So it wasn't hard to discover her daughter, Dahlia. I suppose while I was waiting I had stupid fantasies that she would turn out to be someone important, maybe a famous musician or a celebrity. Something grand like that. Stupid, stupid me." She shook her head and paused to take a sip of her now cold coffee. Getting her composure back.

At that moment the waitress finally returned and they put in orders for muffins and fruit cups and coffee refills.

After the waitress left Morgan continued, "As you all know, I found out the reality pretty quickly. A stripper or at least once a stripper. It wasn't exactly clear how she was living but I knew she had odd waitresssing jobs and also worked part time in a department store. I think she had been a waitress in some of the casinos in town but I wasn't sure how many she still worked in. At least she seemed to be supporting herself. I sent her a letter suggesting we meet. I gave her my phone number and she called me and we agreed to get together. At that time she was working an afternoon shift at Talking Stick casino in Scottsdale so she suggested we meet there after her shift was over."

"It was the envelope of that letter that we found in her house, pushed back into a desk drawer. But the letter itself was missing," Cece interrupted.

Morgan nodded. "It's amazing that you found it and figured out its meaning."

"We were just guessing. But I think we had some kind of sense that it was important."

"Anyway, we met at Talking Stick after her shift was over. That was at the beginning of March. It was a little rocky at first. I think she was embarrassed about her past, how I was born. She said she was raped. She wouldn't tell me who it was. She said she was only fifteen. She cried and said she was sorry. Her mother made her give me up. She wouldn't hear of an abortion so she was sent to Phoenix where I was born. She had no say but in truth she was too young, still a child herself. She begged me to forgive her."

At this point the food arrived and they started to eat, glad for the time out to better absorb the story.

When Morgan resumed, she seemed somehow different as if telling the story was in some strange way changing her. She looked up at the ceiling momentarily, collecting her thoughts. And then continued, "She mentioned Sal Santucci but wouldn't talk about him. I pressed her but she refused to answer. I thought maybe he was the one who raped her but then I didn't think so because her rape had happened years before she started working for him.

"But one thing she said, and it was the last thing she said to me, was that she was going to make it up to me. She had a plan that would bring in a lot of money and she wanted me to have it. Well, I didn't know what to make of that but I was pretty dubious. But that doesn't matter. I just wanted to know her, who she was. If she wasn't someone important, at least I thought she'd be like—well, motherly. I was taken aback. I didn't expect anyone who looked like that. I should have known better. I knew she worked in Vegas clubs, so what did I expect? I don't think I reacted too positively toward her. I was wanting so much to like her but she was so over the top it was hard not to react negatively. Anyway, that was the first and last time I saw her. I can't believe it. I find my mother after all these years and after one meeting she's dead. And to make it worse, if it could be any worse, she wanted to meet with me again just a few days ago on my birthday. And I pretended I couldn't because I had rehearsals. The reality was that I thought it was too weird. I wanted to celebrate the big forty with Vincent and our friends, not someone I really didn't know. I just needed a little more time to absorb it all. So I put it off until this week but now…. It wasn't that I didn't want to see her, it was just so much to process. After all I'm the one who found her. I think I had too much time to imagine what our meeting would be like and when it turned out to be different, I couldn't take it in. I wanted so much for her to be what I wanted.

"Later I was thinking that I hadn't been as welcoming as I might have been. I could tell she was nervous. She talked so fast like she was desperate for me to like her. And it had the opposite effect. If only I'd had more time, maybe we could have been more at ease with each other. Did she die because of me, because she thought I was rejecting her? That's what I'm thinking."

"Oh, no! Surely not." Anne grabbed her hand and squeezed. "That's so awful. To have that happen right when you had a chance to be together after so many years."

"I thought because I was angry at the beginning that she thought I hated her and wouldn't forgive her. That wasn't true but I didn't get a chance to convince her that I didn't think it was her fault. I tried but it was all so much to take in. I don't think I tried hard enough. I just needed a little time to process it all …..and then she was dead. I can't believe it," she repeated and the tears started again. "And on top of all that, I had to learn about her death in the newspaper. No one even knows that I'm her daughter." She stopped for a deep sigh. "Her daughter. I can hardly get my head around that idea, even saying those words. It's all so very, very strange and upsetting. And then you guys show up."

"Bless your heart," Anne murmured. "You have had more than your share of upsets and life-changing events. No one could deal with that easily."

They sat in silence for a few minutes all absorbed in their own thoughts.

"So now you know my story," Morgan finally said.

Cece took a deep breath. "You need to know what we know and I hope it will help. Our book club, the B and B club, that's books and bonding, well, we often read crime books. So when a potential murder happens in our own neighborhood it was pretty much a given we were going to get involved. After all we know the neighborhood and the police don't. They don't live there. So anyway, we have all met your mother or at least seen her since she often attended neighborhood social events. None of us knew her more than in passing but because of a weird fluke we got involved. And this is the part you need to know. The son of one of our B and B'ers was out late the night before the home tour. He saw your mother in the alley behind Sal Santucci's house. He saw her with her cell phone videoing his swim party and then sneaking into his backyard. At least it looked like she was sneaking in."

After describing the incident and how it gave evidence that Dahlia was involved in the possible murder, Cece explained why the police planned on bringing Dahlia in for additional questioning. "She was at the scene of the death according to a reliable witness and she was known to hate Santucci with all the fury of a woman 'scorned.'" Cece made air quotes. "When the police got to her house it was too late. They found her in the old garage behind the house." Cece paused to squeeze Morgan's hand again. "We're so sorry," she said again. "We found out where Dahlia was living and went there to check on what was happening. But everything was pretty much over by then. They were wrapping up the place, keeping onlookers held back by the yellow tape. But the police were already gone.

"The next day we went back, well, just me and Heidi, another B and B'er. We wanted to see for ourselves and find out whatever we could. It was hard to believe that Dahlia would hang herself. She was angry but too full of rage to give it all up. We thought the evidence against her was circumstantial and she maybe could have proved there was reasonable doubt that she was responsible for Santucci's death. She might have been at his house late that night but that didn't mean she killed him. We thought the police just wanted to get the whole case closed but we thought that pinning the murder on Dahlia and then assuming she killed herself in remorse or fear of the consequences, well, that was just a tad too easy an explanation," Cece continued.

"Because the police weren't investigating the scene as a murder, the yellow tape had already been taken down so we, er, er, just poked around and happened to find an open entry in the back of the house." She wiggled her eyebrows at Anne and shrugged. "We searched the house and found a newspaper clipping hidden in an old flour canister in the pantry. That's when we found out about baby Welsh. We put two and two together and thanks to the internet found out that baby Welsh had been put up for adoption. Then I remembered seeing the opened envelope in a desk drawer addressed to Dahlia with a in-town return address. We didn't think too much about until later that evening when we all got together to try to hash out the significance of what we had found. We knew Dahlia by the last name Walker, but by this time we knew her maiden name was Welsh. We thought that it was odd to send a letter to someone who lived so close to you. Plus using her name Welsh. Like maybe an old childhood friend. Anyway we, like I said, we thought it odd to send a letter to someone in town. Normally you'd just text or email. You'd only send a letter to someone you didn't know. Or at least that's what we were thinking.

"We decided that the envelope might be important so we all went back to the house that evening. It was already dark so some of us stayed in one of the cars to watch for any danger and Heidi and I went in another car so we could park out of sight. We went to the back of the house the same as we had before. We climbed through the window again and grabbed the envelope. Then Stacey and Stephanie, who were lookouts in the car in front of the house, called my cell and warned us that someone had approached the house and appeared to be going around to the backyard. They're B and B'ers also, Stacey and Stephanie."

"That was me!" Morgan interrupted. "I had just found out about her dying and I wanted to be there. I had never even had time to go to her house, to know where she lived. I had her address and I just wanted to be near her. Maybe it was weird but I couldn't help it."

"That's good to know. We were pretty freaked out that we'd be caught or maybe it was someone dangerous. Glad it was you!

"We had tracked you down and knew that you were likely still living in Phoenix and so it was just a guess that maybe that letter was from you. We didn't know your adopted name. A wild guess but we thought it was a lead that we should investigate. So all that led up to our going to the Egyptian and seeing you play."

Morgan shook her head in amazement. "I can't believe you guys. You're like the best detectives ever. I had no idea when you came backstage to visit that all this was happening. Wow."

"We figured that even if we were wrong, it would be fun to go to the Egyptian. We all wanted to see it anyway since it got a lot of press when it opened not long ago. We were undecided about who you were, so Anne and I decided to return. When we heard your beautiful sad song we thought it had to have been inspired by what had happened. And so here we are!"

The three of them sat silently. So much to take in.

"But Dahlia, …er…my mother, do you think she didn't commit suicide? How else can you explain it?"

"Remember, there was a suicide note but only one word 'sorry' and it was written in block letters so it would be impossible to identify the handwriting. We didn't find anything that looked like a note had been written. No note paper or pens lying about. So this one word note didn't seem right for the place. Like someone put it there and it was not written by someone who was planning to end her life. That doesn't prove anything but it adds to the doubt about what actually happened. Like we said, we think the police just wanted to wrap up both the Santucci death and hers as settled and proved."

Cece continued, "It's possible that she was murdered. After all she was there at the party that night and obviously she was there for a reason or she wouldn't have been sneaking in from the alley. All the 'girls' from the club were leaving according to Heidi's son so what could have happened then? Maybe she knew what really happened to Santucci and was going to go to the police about it. We know she had her cell phone and was filming when she snuck in. What if she filmed some kind of confrontation that led to his death? If so, the murderer would have to stop her."

"But that would all be on her phone, wouldn't it?" Morgan asked.

"True, but where is her phone?" Anne and Cece looked at each other with a start.

"Exactly, *where* is her phone?" Cece continued. "We didn't find a phone either in the garage or in her house. The police had already been there so no doubt they would have taken it if they found it. When they first investigated Santucci's death, they didn't know about Dahlia's being there. That was discovered a week later and before they had time to bring her in for more questioning she was discovered dead. Another thing we thought suspicious was the presence of two glasses in the sink. It maybe didn't mean anything but it suggests that someone else might have been at the house. Everything else in the house was neat and tidy. Everything in its place, all put away. But those two glasses."

"Wouldn't a murderer know to clean everything up? You know, not leave any evidence of any kind," Morgan said.

"Yes, probably, but that's assuming he—or—she was a real killer. Maybe it involved someone who wasn't a killer, who wouldn't really think of all the things a real criminal would think of."

"Wouldn't the police have tested the two glasses?" Morgan asked.

"We asked that same question but apparently they didn't. All we know is that they have shelved the investigation so at this point it's all conjecture. So whatever happened is going to be hard to prove."

"I'm so sorry, Morgan. I can't begin to understand what you must be going through. I think we, at least us book clubbers, need to follow up on the cell phone. Plus, I don't know what's happened with your mother's house. It is a rental we know, so all her personal things would still be there."

"Do you think I could have those things? At least I would have some way of knowing who she was if I could see what she lived with. It didn't seem like she had any other children or any kind of family. My DNA search didn't come up with any other close relatives."

"Her belongings should be yours," Anne emphasized.

"But no one even knows she's my mother. I barely know it myself." Morgan glanced at her watch. "I'm sorry, ladies, but Vincent and I have a rehearsal scheduled before our next performance. He doesn't even know where I am. I'd better be going."

"We understand. Let's plan on getting back together soon. I think we can arrange for you to get into your mother's house. We'll work on it and let you know as soon as we can."

CHAPTER TWENTY-TWO

Monday night was the first time all the B and B'ers could get together. Maddie's house had the front door open for everyone with Daisy sitting on the porch as the dog welcoming committee. Cece had left Nicky behind despite his protests. As the door shut on him, he had run to the dining room window overlooking the front patio to watch Cece walking toward the street. He had let out such a mournful yowl just as the train whistle also filled the air of the silent evening. Yowling dogs, faraway trains, all so fraught…fraught with what?

All the way to Maddie's house Cece felt a strange foreboding. Maybe George was right. They should have stayed out of it all. What good had it done? They hadn't accomplished anything. She quickly shook that thought away, remembering Morgan. They had helped Morgan. Without them, she would have known almost nothing of her biological mother and she might even have continued to be filled with regret and guilt. No, they had helped. Whatever else they had done, they had helped Morgan.

With that thought, Cece entered Maddie's house. Everyone was gathered in the front room. "Over here," Heidi called, patting a spot on the chintz covered sofa. Cece wiggled in between Heidi and Anne and sat back.

"Go ahead and tell them what happened when we met Morgan," Cece said, seeing that everyone was there and seated.

Anne recounted their breakfast meeting at the First Watch. Then everyone looked around at each other. "What now?"

"For starters," Heidi chimed in. "I'll find out who owns Dahlia's house. We can get permission to get in so Morgan can collect whatever personal items she might want. I think that will help her find some closure on this whole unfortunate….uh, what to call it? A mess."

"Good idea," Maddie said. "I'll see what I can find out about the items the police took when they took Dahlia to the morgue. I think her belongings will stay at the morgue until someone is entitled to claim them. I'll especially try to find out if Dahlia's phone is there. If so it should have been analyzed but if they were so willing to wrap up the investigation, who knows what they did or didn't do."

After hearing about the meeting between Dahlia and Morgan and the struggles Morgan was having with all the new and unexpected events in her life, they all were curious about Morgan and decided they should visit the Egyptian often as long as she was playing there. They would be her little fan club and maybe help her get established in the arts district.

By the next morning Heidi had located the owner of the Story rental where Dahlia had lived. Hillary Gaynor owned a number of rentals in the area and was also a Realtor with Russ Lyon Sotheby's Realty. As soon as she heard of her tenant's death, she had her property manager put a lockbox on the house in anticipation of its being cleared out and rented again shortly. Heidi knew Hillary at least socially and she occasionally had business relations with Hillary's real estate company. Hillary Gaynor, unfortunately was on an extended trip to Europe but, once contacted, was eager to cooperate to get the house cleared out and put back on the market. It was only because of her trip that the process had been delayed. Generally, she liked to meet new tenants in person but of course had not anticipated having an empty rental during her trip. Once Heidi explained the events that led up to the house being vacated, she was more than happy to let Heidi bring Morgan in. She gave Heidi the number of her manager for her rentals, saying he was authorized to take care of anything during her absence.

Heidi quickly got hold of him and he agreed to put a lockbox on the front door so Heidi could get in.

The next morning Morgan met Heidi at the front of the Story house. Morgan had already pulled up and parked in front of the house and was sitting in her car, staring at the house. Cece had wanted to come along so she was there also. Since Morgan had only met Cece at First Watch but not Heidi, she got a quick update on Heidi's involvement in finding Dahlia's house and how she and Cece had been the ones to sneak in the back window the week before.

"This is going to be strange," Morgan commented. "But thanks, Heidi. I do want to know my mother as best I can at this point. Seeing her things might help."

Heidi punched in the lockbox code and opened the door, pushing aside a pile of mail on the floor.

"That beats climbing in the back window," Cece said, looking a little sheepish.

"Really? You two climbed in a window in the back?" She shook her head with amazement.

"I didn't, just her," Cece pointed an accusing finger at Heidi.

"Ha, ha," Heidi retorted.

"You two could be cat burglars!"

"Ouch! Don't say that! We actually did debate whether or not we should break in. But it was decided that we weren't really breaking in since the house was empty and we weren't stealing anything *and* we knew Dahlia, so we were just doing a favor."

Morgan gave her a questioning look, eyebrows furled. "Funny how it sort of turned out that way whether intended or not."

"Right! We knew of course what we were doing was questionable but we just made a feeble rationalization. The end justifies the means sort of thing."

"Sure! Okay by me," Morgan smiled at them, the two guilty break and enterers.

The three filed into the small living, dining room combination. Morgan scanned the room silently, scowling ever so slightly. Her eyes traced the framed photos and memorabilia hanging on the walls, undoubtedly from clubs where Dahlia had worked.

"All these photos. It makes her work look somehow glamorous. The glitzy surface to a life much less nice, at least the way Dahlia described it the other day."

"Let us show you where we found the birth announcement clipping," Heidi said, pointing the way. They entered the kitchen and went to the pantry to retrieve the flour canister. "It was in here," she said, pulling open the door and reaching up to the high shelf where the set of canisters still rested. "I bet these tins haven't been touched in years."

"What on earth made you think to look in there?" Morgan asked.

"Our grandmothers," Cece laughed. "That's where women in their day hid their emergency money so they would never be left stranded no matter what happened."

"An ATM doesn't do the same thing?" Morgan questioned.

"It would but where were their ATM's?"

"Right. No ATMs. It's hard to imagine a time when your money, at least if you had any, wasn't almost instantly available."

"Yep. A lot has changed in the last fifty years or so. That's for sure," Cece nodded.

Morgan continued through the house. She opened the bedroom closet doors and surveyed its contents of sequined tops, boas, crazy captain's hats. Costumes.

"Why did she keep all this stuff?" Morgan wondered. "She wasn't performing any more. How strange."

Cece remembered how she and Heidi had made fun of all of the costumes but she kept her mouth shut. Morgan didn't need to have any more unpleasant thoughts about her mother.

Morgan closed the closet door. Her mother's clothing was not anything she wanted but she did take some of the pictures and photos from the walls. They had brought shopping bags to take the things out. Once she had taken everything that seemed to have meaning, she turned to look down at all the mail lying in the narrow hallway under the mail slot in the front door. "It's nice that these old houses have mail slots built into the house itself so you don't have to go outside to a mailbox. Nothing to get overstuffed if you're out of town." She started picking up the mail and sorting it into piles on a small hall table. "I wonder if I should get the mail delivery stopped. I don't think I can even prove I'm Dahlia's daughter and I don't know if just anyone could do it."

Heidi had brought a shopping bag that she now held open so Morgan could shovel the mail inside. "It looks like it's a lot of advertising and junk mail. And some bills. APS and Chase Bank. I guess I'm the one who should take care of all this." Morgan sighed and slowly shook her head as she surveyed the pile of correspondence. "Wait a minute," she exclaimed suddenly. "This one is interesting. Might be important." She picked up a medium sized package. A small somewhat bulky mailing envelope had been covered by mailing flyers. Morgan peered at the label which was addressed to Dahlia. The return address was a lab in California. Heidi and Cece came over to peer over her shoulder.

"I wonder what that's all about?" Cece murmured. "Are you going to open it?"

"I have a creepy feeling about this. I don't know why but…." She started to pull the turned over flap loose. Reaching in, she pulled out a small bundle wrapped in white paper. Undoing the tape and unrolling the paper produced a toothbrush, an old toothbrush. Morgan held her breath. She extracted the printed papers that accompanied the toothbrush. "I know what this is," she said, her voice low and uncertain. "It's a DNA test result. I know because that's what I got and that's what I used to find her."

"But who's it for?" Cece asked. "This isn't the ordinary 23and-Me or Ancestry. They don't take toothbrushes, they take swabs and they don't send them back. This is something else."

Morgan unfolded the paperwork and started reading to herself. "It's for Sal Santucci. It's his family tree based on the sample taken from his toothbrush. The request was dated March 17, 2025 and they received it three days later." Morgan read through the lab's report, noting they were a speciality service that provided results much faster than the more common DNA companies.

Suddenly she stopped, drawing in a gasp. "I'm listed as a close relation. Oh my god! A daughter!! I sent in my own DNA sample when I wanted to find my mother so my DNA is in the data base. That Sal Santucci, the one who was killed a week or so ago, is my father!!" Morgan dropped to the floor amidst the pile of letters, holding the paper with a look of absolute astonishment on her face. "I'm speechless!"

CHAPTER TWENTY-THREE

They all sat down on the floor in stunned silence, the letters and flyers strewn around them.

"But….but….they're both dead." Morgan shook her head slowly, color draining from her face. "I find both my biological parents just weeks apart and they're both gone. How could that happen? I can't think straight."

"Wait a minute." Cece held up a hand. Morgan and Heidi turned to her, eyes wide. "This report is for Sal Santucci but it was Dahlia who sent it in. If Santucci was interested in his DNA, he would have done it himself and he would have done the usual cheek swap and sent it in to the usual places….the places that only do cheek swabs and not hair or toothbrushes. That's what the police often use for DNA samples but they have their own labs of course. So how come Dahlia is sending in Santucci's toothbrush?"

"Because she knew Santucci was the father of her baby! You!" Cece looked at Morgan. "But when she was fifteen she couldn't prove it. He was much older but anyway there's no evidence that Dahlia or her mother tried to make Santucci responsible."

"She was still a child and Santuccii would have been committing a crime. So he probably just left Dahlia and her parents to deal with it on their own."

"Not so unusual, unfortunately, at that time. No one could prove anything then."

"No wonder Dahlia hated him so much. He gets her pregnant when she's only fifteen, skips out but hires her three or four years later to work in his strip clubs. I wonder if she thought maybe she could win him over."

"Or win him back!" Heidi butted in. "Maybe she wasn't really raped. Maybe she thought she was in love with him. Wouldn't be the first fifteen-year-old to think something goofy like that. So years later, maybe she convinced herself to believe him when he said he would marry her and build a house for them on his and her mother's properties. Then she finds out about you, Morgan! You are their child together. It must have seemed like fate. Maybe she thought that at last they would be together—that Santucci would acknowledge you as their daughter and you all would be a family."

"That seems like a stretch," Cece broke in. "He wasn't considered by anyone to be a nice guy. Very angry all the time. Always fighting with people, creating a maelstrom of chaos wherever he was." Cece turned to Morgan, "I'm sorry to have to say such negative things about the person you just found out to be your father. I wish I had something good to say."

Morgan's shoulders slumped and she sat back on her heels. "It's all a bit too much. That's for sure."

Cece pushed herself up from the floor, dusting off her jeans. "Get up, you two. We have work to do!"

Morgan heaved a long sigh, a dazed look filling her eyes. "Work?" she mumbled. "What work?" She pulled herself upright along with Heidi.

"You need an attorney, for starters. You're the heir of a

wealthy man! Hang on to those papers like your life depends on it. He may have other children and even spouses for all I know. I think it might be a circus! But it's a circus that you're now part of!"

A small "oh" from Morgan. "I need to talk to Vincent!"

"If you're the only next of kin, can you claim your mother's body?"

Morgan stiffened. "But—but, do I want to claim her body? I mean, have a funeral and all that? It's too much. I don't know what to do," she nearly wailed.

"Get an attorney to represent you. That's the first thing. You need legal advice before you do anything on your own, don't you think?" Cece continued. "One of our group works as a clerk for City Hall. She knows all the attorneys in town. She can get some recommendations for you. But only if you want that, of course. You can no doubt find someone yourself."

"No, no. I want you to help. I really don't know anyone in town. I have no idea who would be good. Why would I ever think I needed a lawyer?"

"Funny how things happen," Heidi said. "In a day or two your whole life has been turned upside down."

Morgan nodded.

"Listen to this, guys." Cece caught their attention. "Dahlia sent in that toothbrush on Monday the day after the home tour. So I'm thinking that if Dahlia sent in Santucci's toothbrush for testing and was waiting for the results that she already knew, results that would prove Santucci was the father of her daughter, why would she kill herself? She would want to know for sure and she would have the proof to go after Santucci, maybe not for child support obviously, but for something. Something that would help Morgan. Remember, Morgan," she said, searching Morgan's face. "She told you she was going to help you *financially*. And if she could help you that would be a bond between you two that might make up for the years of separation. I bet she was thinking like that. And that's not the thinking of someone who doesn't want to live anymore."

There was a silent pause to take that idea in and roll it around.

Finally Cece continued, "Of course! That's why she snuck into Santucci's backyard the night of his swim party. She probably knew he'd be drunk and distracted and thought she could get in the house unseen and find something with his DNA. What better than a toothbrush?"

Heidi nodded energetically. "Yes, of course that's right. So she's in the house when all the girls are leaving but she might have waited, hiding, and seen something else. Maybe she saw the murderer."

"We're not sure he was murdered, right?" Cece looked at them questioningly.

"Whatever happened, she must have seen it. And we know how much she used her cell phone so what if she saw what really happened that night after everyone left and got it on video. That would be pretty impressive. We know now that her cell phone is missing. Maddie confirmed that. She checked the medical examiner's office and got the public records for the things that were taken from the morgue. Since the cause of death was ruled 'indeterminate' at that time, all items were sent to the police station to keep in case the status of the death might change and become a crime. I contacted the police and they didn't have a cell phone at the station. Apparently the police searched her house and no cell phone was found. Who doesn't have a cell phone? Dahlia certainly had one, so where is it? That seems to be the key to this whole mystery. Where's the cell phone?"

CHAPTER TWENTY-FOUR

That night at dinner Cece filled George in on all the recent events. "You ladies know how to butt in. That's for sure," he commented as he finished off the last bite of a chicken taco.

"Don't be such a grump. We may have gotten Dahlia's daughter an inheritance. Who knew? And I might add Morgan is nothing like her mother. She's very down to earth, no phony showoffness."

"Showoffness?" queried George, quirking an eyebrow in her direction.

"You know what I mean. She's very low key and sweet and has such a beautiful voice. And what music talent! Just shows all that superficial in-your-face sexuality is not in your genes. They're both performers, but what a difference!"

"Not to change the subject, Cece, but did you hear the local news earlier?"

"No, I missed it. Texting and cooking dinner." She smiled sweetly.

"The homeless camp has finally been cleared out. Everyone's gone. Everything's gone. Just a little trash left behind. There was a camera crew from local news filming the evacuation and the mound of trash left behind. I think you ladies will be relieved at that, eh?"

"I guess so but, of course, where are they going? They're not going to just disappear or move to Florida to sit on the beach. Encanto Park is too open and too appealing with all its trees and the lagoon. They might not set up encampments nearby for a while but it's always a draw. So the day people and the night people. And the night people? We may not see them but they seem to always be with us. They're in constant flux. Forming new groups and splitting off to reemerge somewhere else. But not going away. And speaking of night people, I read the neighborhood emails this afternoon and someone posted a video from their side porch security camera that was recorded at four o'clock this morning and guess what was on it?"

"Homeless people skulking about?" George volunteered with an innocent grin.

"No, the ocelot! It's still in the neighborhood but north, closer to the park. So we still have to be extra careful with Nicky. An ocelot could jump our back fence in a heartbeat."

They both looked down at Nicky who had moved to his usual place by George's side waiting for a hand with a snack to appear by his nose. His ears pricked up on hearing his name. He had been stretched out under George's chair waiting for his usual purloined tidbits of whatever was on the table but now he had moved out from under the chair and was sitting up at attention.

"It's surprising that it's still in the area considering how far they're known to travel. So I guess that means it's a female. Or at least according to Fred Spencer," Cece commented while adding a sprinkle of grated cheese to her taco.

"Who's Fred?" George folded up his napkin and placed it and his elbows on the table and looked at Cece with interest.

"The wildlife biologist who has the certified habitat yard on Palmcroft Drive circle. I bet he's worried the ocelot might show up on his property. He's got all those koi and mallards in his swimming pool/pond. And he's the one who was so mad at Santucci for even owning it. Funny, isn't it?"

"Not so funny if the ocelot starts eating people's pets. Their cats and dogs. Or their ducks or the ducks on the lagoon in the park. Nobody would be laughing over that!" George declared with an emphatic tap of his fingers on the table.

Nicky jumped up, resting his paws on George's leg. Cats! Dogs! Eating cats and dogs! Something bad was going on. He was on alert! He looked up at George's face and saw nothing but worry. He wanted answers.

"Ha! At least it's not the immigrants! If immigrants or the homeless for that matter were trying to eat the ducks in the lagoon and the bunnies on the golf course, they'd have to fight off the bobcats and coyotes first! Now that would be a battle to watch. If they lost, they might have a go at Fluffy and Fido!! We don't want to have to deal with that, like the people in that poor little town in Ohio!"

"Very funny," George grumbled and got up to take his dinner dishes into the kitchen.

CHAPTER TWENTY-FIVE

The next evening the B and B book clubbers held another emergency meeting at Anne's house. That seemed the appropriate place since Anne's backyard backed up to the wall that separated the homeless encampment from the neighborhood. Now at last it was an empty field.

But Maddie was, of course, the one they turned to after the trip to Dahlia's house to collect her things had been thoroughly explained. Maddie knew all the inside gossip about the best attorneys in town. And any attorney for Morgan would be dealing with a claimant for an estate that included the Santucci mansion and the clubs in Scottsdale and Vegas not to mention any others that might exist. Any lawyer would consider representing such a claimant a plum job.

"I think we've done our best with the whole situation of Dahlia and her newly found daughter. Now it's up to Morgan to pursue whatever avenue she wishes to take. It's not like she's a motherless child. She is just as knowledgeable as any of us, for heavens sake," Maddie reminded them.

"Good point," Stephanie agreed. "But the other part of the Dahlia thing is, was she murdered or did she commit suicide?

Finding that out is our goal, isn't it? To solve the murder, if it is one. We know the police are no longer investigating. Her body was released to one of those funeral homes that takes in indigent people, unclaimed bodies, and arranges for their cremation. It's too late for anyone to examine the body. And how thorough was the medical examiner's autopsy? Was there even an autopsy? If the cause of death was ruled a suicide, there would be little reason to do an autopsy. Plus the medical examiner's office was closed for months for remodeling and updating. How would that effect their work?"

"By the way," Cece interjected. "Morgan texted me yesterday that she was going to claim her mother's body and have her cremated. She said she couldn't just let her mother be buried anonymously in some pauper's grave. She has an attorney now and she's helping her with the process."

"That's good. As for us, there are still too many questions we can't answer," Anne added. "But the real question is—could she have been murdered? Obviously a murderer would have a hard time making someone hang herself. Even a strong man and a weak woman. There would be signs of a struggle that would be hard to overlook."

"What if she was drunk or drugged? Or strangled first? Then her body could have been strung up and it would look like suicide."

They looked at each other. That was possible, wasn't it? They nodded pretty much in unison.

"Or," broke in Stephanie. "What about a *garrot*? A rope *garrot* that would leave the same kind of rope burns on the neck that a noose would leave."

They all looked a little startled. Images of a garroting flashed

through their minds. Gruesome.

"That would mean a vicious murderer is now loose in our community," Cece said carefully.

"If she was murdered, no matter how, we have a vicious murderer loose. That's just one reason this suicide, death, whatever it is, needs to be solved for once and for all."

Group nodding of heads.

"So what now?" Anne finally asked.

That was the question that none of them seemed able to answer.

The following morning Cece was awakened early, the sun not yet rising over the horizon. Resigned to not falling back asleep, she got up quietly to not disturb George and went into the kitchen to start a pot of coffee. She slipped out the front door to the driveway to retrieve the newspaper. A stiff wind had picked up, a change after so many days of balmy weather.

Cece sighed. Not a surprise, she thought. There's always at least one more cold front moving through before the heat of summer set in for good. She pulled her bathrobe a little tighter and looked up, searching for the moon still bright in the early morning sky. A bat suddenly swooped across her vision. Then another and another. The summer bat migration, she thought. She shook her head, thinking of the night creatures—the bats, the cats, the predators, both animal and human. How could a neighborhood as calm and settled as Palmcroft overlay a dark underbelly of activities so contrary to the feeling of security that most of the residents assumed was normal? So much easier to ignore the night and whatever mysteries it held. Focus on the sunshine. Yes, that was the way to go. She was happy not to have security cameras around her house. Did she really want to see who or what was lurking about her walls in the wee hours of night? NO!

She picked up the folded newspaper just as the sprinkler system spurted on, startling her. Water, she contemplated. Wherever there was water there would be life, all life both good and bad. That couldn't be more true than here in the desert. Artificially produced water from sprinklers, swimming pools, fish ponds, the lagoon in the park. It was the draw.

She brought the paper into the house and traipsed into the kitchen to fill her cup with coffee and add a splash of cream and a cube of sugar. She settled down on the sofa, sipping her coffee while reading the paper. That was a tradition she would never give up. The news was just not the same on a computer or iPad. Only the newspaper would do. It made Cece feel her age but she didn't care. Her phone was charging on the table next to her coffee cup when it pinged a message. Glancing over, Cece noticed it was from the neighborhood email.

She reached over to open her phone and click on the email. Ironically just posted was a security camera photo showing the shadowy stooped figure of a woman banging on a gate. The caption read, "Have you seen this woman? She's trying to get into my yard."

Cece squinted at the photo. It was blurry in the darkness of the alley gate but it was clearly a woman. She was wearing a long sleeved black teeshirt and khaki pants. Black socks and black rubber sandals covered her feet. But it was that dark red hair twisted into a sloppy bun with the incongruent fake flower stuck haphazardly into it that made the recognition certain. Carrie! What was she up to?

Cece checked the posting and knew the approximate location of the alley where Carrie was. Not far. She quickly pulled on a pair of sweat pants and a sweater and headed out the door. As she started to pull open the front door, she felt a bump on her leg. There was Nicky looking ready to go. He might as well have been yelling 'take me, take me.'

"Okay, sweet guy." She grabbed the halter and leash off the coat rack, slipped it over his head and together they slipped out the front door, Cece closing it softy behind them.

They hurried up Eleventh Avenue under the mellow light of the street lamps. She turned west on Palm Lane until reaching Twelfth Avenue where it bordered Encanto Park. A sharp right turn and they were mid-block at the entrance of the alley. She hesitated, pretty sure that it was the alley in the email. This was surely where Carrie had been. Had she had time to get away? Cece and Nicky entered the alley away from the shine of the street lights and the darkness intensified. Shadows of trees overhanging block walls, trash cans and occasional belongings no longer wanted cast strange shadows. Cece was beginning to chastise herself for the madness of thinking chasing around after Carrie would accomplish anything of worth. I am an idiot. She silently fumed. "Why didn't you stop me, Nicky? You're smarter than I am!" she whispered.

Nicky had been pulling at his leash, excited to find so many new smells to investigate. He suddenly stiffened, peering into a gloomy recession in a wooden wall. A dark green city garbage can was pushed against the wall, the top raised just enough for a pair of khaki clad legs to hang down from the rim. The legs slowly descended toward the ground. A black shirt and a messy head came next. She came fully into view and twisted around, hearing Nicky's low growl. She held a large section of a pizza in one hand. She saw Nicky first and then raised her head to stare at Cece.

Her entire face scrunched into an angry scowl. "You," she growled. "You dog lady. You devil dog." She pointed her free hand at Nicky.

"We're not here to bother you, " Cece started uncertainly. "Are you hungry?"

Carrie peered at Cece before waving the pizza in the air. "It's the cats," she whispered in that voice that Cece remembered from their earlier meeting. That soft frightening whisper. "It's the cats. My cats." She turned away from Cece and Nicky and started down the alley heading toward Holly Street and the park. Then unexpectedly she turned back, motioning to Cece. "Come."

Carrie approached the end of the alley where a construction chain link fence surrounded the grounds of a large two-story house. Cece recognized the house, one of several large properties in the neighborhood being gutted for total remodeling. A huge pile of construction debris ran from the alley to halfway along the side of the property. Two-by-fours, drywall panels, carpeting piled helter-skelter into a mountain of rubbish. Carrie stopped abruptly, holding out an arm as if to prevent Cece from moving forward.

She turned back to Cece. "Keep that devil dog away. Away."

Cece gripped Nicky's leash pulling him back behind her legs. "He's okay. I won't let him go. What is it? What's there?"

Carrie crept closer to the fence. At the ground level a few feet of the chain link had been twisted by a protruding rafter lifting it no more than a foot above the ground. Under the rafter, a narrow opening appeared dark in the pale dawn light. Studs angled upward, partially covered by what was once wall-to-wall carpeting that flopped over the small opening. Carrie moved slowly forward crouching low to place the slice of pizza on the ground. She slid it under the chain link toward the opening. "Back, back." She rose slowly, twisting to face Cece and pushing her arm out as if she could physically push Cece away.

Nicky was frozen in place, trembling with what? Rage? Excitement? Cece didn't know but it was clear something living was under that mountain of rubble. Nicky started to growl, a low rumble. Cece pulled him away despite his digging in his front paws, skidding in protest.

"We're going. You don't have to worry. Nicky can't get loose. See. I've got him." She looked hopefully at Carrie, realizing for the first time that the dawn was slowly transforming the night sky into day. She backed up, pulling Nicky along with his front legs still stiff and resistant.

"My cats," Carrie whispered, glancing sideways at Cece, and still frowning suspiciously. "My cats. My black cat, Spot. Spot, I call her. Little spots." She laughed a soft cackle. "You help. The men, oh, they're coming with their backhoes, their tractors."

Suddenly Cece understood. Whatever was under that pile, it would soon lose its home. Spot, black spot, little spots? Cece wondered. Could it be the ocelot? She looked black, at least in the dark, and spotted and she was seen on camera just the other day in this area. Surely that was it! But the next thought was more unsettling. Debris never stayed long in the neighborhood remodels. This construction pile no doubt only existed because the sheer amount of trash would have overwhelmed a street side dumpster. How long had that pile been there? She tried to remember. She didn't drive on that street often so she wasn't sure but she thought it had been there at least a week and maybe longer.

She turned to Carrie. "Is it the ocelot?" Small squeaking sounds came from under the pile. Something living was definitely there.

But Carrie had turned away and was shuffling back into the shadows of the alley as the neighborhood gradually emerged from the night darkness. The night people fading away with the night itself. Cece headed for home, pulling Nicky along.

CHAPTER TWENTY-SIX

By the time Cece and Nicky got to their front door, clouds were scudding across the sky. The bright pink sunrise had faded into a dour grey and the newly budding elms were swaying wildly in the rising wind. Cece shuddered, hurrying to get inside the warm house.

George was sitting in the living room reading the paper and sipping coffee. "Trying to beat the storm?" he asked.

"I guess. Sorry but I didn't want to wake you and the sunrise was so beautiful I thought it would be fun to have an early morning walk." Only a partial lie, she thought. More a lie of omission rather than an out-and-out lie. And those hardly counted.

"That's okay. When I saw Nicky was gone, then it was pretty obvious what you were up to. Meet anyone interesting?"

Cece frowned. Did she really want to get into the whole homeless thing? George had been upset that she and Anne had visited the encampment and he was certainly relieved when the whole lot of them had been cleared out. She hesitated, and was about to answer when she realized that George had already turned his attention back to the sports section.

Ok, that takes care of that, she thought. She unhitched Nicky's halter and hung it and his leash on the coat rack. Getting another cup of coffee she settled back onto the sofa next to George and glanced at her watch. Seven ten. She needed to call Liberty Wildlife Center but they weren't open until nine. She hated to wait but it was unlikely anything would change in just a few hours. She reminded herself that ocelots are nocturnal. What if she had kittens? Was the sound she heard the sound of kittens mewing? Whatever it was had stayed hidden. Besides she wasn't totally sure what was living under that pile of rubble. Maybe a stray dog. They were sometimes abandoned in Encanto Park by heartless owners. But it could have been the ocelot? Carrie said a black cat. Ocelots aren't black but at night they could look black. It was possible. But clearly, Carrie wasn't the best source of information. Or……maybe she was.

Liberty Wildlife Center opened at nine. Cece got them on the phone almost immediately after they opened.

"I think I may know where that escaped ocelot is," she told the volunteer who answered the phone. "Is Mr. Nugent in? I'd like to speak to him about the information I have." She was put on hold for what seemed an interminable amount of time until finally Gary Nugent came on the line. Cece explained what had happened that morning and as she talked she began to doubt her sureness that it really was the ocelot that was hiding under a pile of construction rubble. It sounded crazy. And…. that her informant, if you could call her that, was a homeless lady who was almost nonverbal. It really sounded off the wall. By the time she finished she was blushing with embarrassment.

"Hummmm." Gary Nugent mumbled into the phone. Hopefully he didn't think she was nuts. Maybe he was thinking about the ocelot or maybe he was thinking about how to get rid of the crazy lady. He continued, "The ocelot has been spotted in that vicinity rather recently. It's possible that she was pregnant and looking for a place to have her litter. This is the season for it."

Cece nodded automatically although obviously Gary couldn't see her. "Plus," she added. "I saw that security camera footage of her from the other day and I looked closely at it and I think she was limping. I think she's hurt."

"Well, then. Give me a few minutes to make arrangements and I'll call you right back. The problem is Liberty Wildlife doesn't rehabilitate larger mammals. I'll have to contact Arizona Fish and Game. We sometimes collaborate, so we'll certainly help out if needed. But leave it to me and we will see what's going on. It is extremely important to capture the ocelot before it is too late for her. Surviving in a huge city is almost impossible for any predator other then coyotes and sometimes bobcats. But we won't know if it is her or not if we don't check it out."

Cece gave a description of the location and was assured a van with a crew would be there within an hour. She was thanked by him and as Cece hung up she wondered just what had happened. If only animals could talk. She would love to hear that story!

An Arizona Fish and Game van showed up less than an hour later just about on the dot. Cece had driven her car to the intersection near the construction site. She sipped on a travel cup of coffee while waiting. When she saw the van, she got out of her car and motioned the van toward the construction site. The van parked at the edge of the street.

Two young people, a man and a woman, climbed out. They wore heavy jackets and thick leather gloves. They introduced themselves quickly and Cece explained the circumstances and why she suspected that she had found the ocelot den. She led them to the edge of the fencing and showed them the place with the lifted chain link and the dark recess under the layers of carpet.

"You need to get back in your car," the young woman said.

Reluctantly Cece turned back and got in her car. At least she had a perfect view to watch what was going to happen.

After some initial probing with a long pole ending in a loop with a pull rope to tighten it, the head of a very angry ocelot appeared at the entrance of the opening. That was just enough to allow the rope to slip over her head. Once tightened, she was pulled from the den and quickly deposited into a waiting opened up cage in the back of the van. She was not happy. The woman who was considerably smaller than her companion crawled under the fencing and disappeared head first into the opening. A minute late she came out with a squirming bundle of fur. Two more tries produced two more.

"Three kittens!" Cece exclaimed. Once the ocelot was in the cage she had climbed from her car and come closer to watch the rest of the rescue. "That's amazing!"

"Yes, that's as large a litter as ocelots have. She was lucky to have that many. Maybe she was well cared for during her gestation period."

Cece thought of Sal Santucci. Did he really care for this beautiful creature? Maybe he did. What a strange man. She realized she knew almost nothing of him. And yet the book club was totally invested in finding his murderer. Or at least determining how he died. She glanced at her watch. Almost ten-thirty. She had to call Stacey to let her know that the ocelot was not only safe but a mother as well. Ollie B would be ecstatic!

She phoned Stacey while she was still sitting at the construction site watching the van retreating around a corner. "Hi Stacey. You won't believe what just happened. I'm in my car over near Monte Vista Street and Twelfth. Have you seen the big house that's being gutted over there? Anyway there's a huge pile of construction rubble and guess what was found underneath that huge pile?"

Cece filled Stacey in on the whole adventure and the ultimate capture of the ocelot with her kittens. "She's wounded also. Her paw is bloody and partially mangled. Maybe infected. She could have had a run-in with a big dog or a coyote or even hurt it just trying to survive in this crazy city. The vets at Fish and Game will probably be able to assess the damage and figure out what caused it. Liberty Wildlife Center of course couldn't do anything for her themselves but they helped coordinate the transfer. She will go to the Southwest Wildlife Conservation Center in Scottsdale. They're the ones that treat larger mammals. They'll care for her until she can be transferred to a permanent home. They said that unfortunately she can never be released into the wild since she's probably lived her entire life in captivity. We pretty much knew that already. But they did say that once they're older, it might be a different story for her kittens. I'm not sure what will happen to them. Anyway, it's really amazing that all these organizations operate to protect our wildlife. I bet ninety-nine percent of people in Phoenix have no idea that they even exist.

"Also the people who caught her said we could call later this afternoon and probably get an update on her condition. I bet Ollie B would be pretty excited to hear it."

They agreed to call just as soon as Ollie B got home from school.

Cece was totally charged up. She drove home smiling happily to herself. As she pulled into the driveway, she saw George waiting at the door.

"What happened. Did you find it?" he called before she was even out of the car.

"Yep. Sure did and she had kittens!" Cece answered as she climbed out of the car and headed for the front patio.

Nicky had run to the door and was waiting anxiously when Cece came in. He sensed the excitement and started jumping against Cece's leg. "No, Nick. Calm down. You knew what was there, didn't you? You smart, smart boy!" Nicky's stubby tail was wagging so hard, his whole backside gyrated with it. "You are the one who found her! Well, maybe Carrie too."

"That's great. So now they'll be taken care of. But what will happen to them all?" George asked as Cece went into the kitchen for a fresh cup of coffee.

"I'm going to call either Fish and Game or Southwest Wildlife this afternoon to find out more. Hopefully we'll know then. Also I think I should go over to Fred's and let him know about the rescue. I think he'll be really happy about it. Do you want to come?"

"I would but I already scheduled a meeting with the draftsman that's probably going to take hours. Plus, I have to drive to his office and he lives all the way out in Buckeye. That's going to take all afternoon I'm sure."

"You might not miss much. I don't know how much they'll know in just a few hours. But anyway, I'll fill you in when I get home from Fred's. I've got to call Heidi. I think she'll want to go too. Fred's a little unfriendly so I like to have company when I'm around him."

"That's the wildlife biologist guy?"

"Right. He's the one that was threatening Santucci, saying that he'd report him for keeping a protected animal. It happened at a board meeting a few months ago. I don't know how he knew Santucci had an ocelot but apparently he did. No one else seemed to know about it. Anyway, it was an ugly confrontation in the parking lot and a bunch of people saw it. So Fred should be happy that the ocelot has been found and will no doubt have a happier home than she did at Santucci's."

"Is Stacey going too?"

"No, she has some jobs to take care of while Ollie B's in school. So she's out. Anyway it won't take long to tell Fred. He's only a few blocks away. And that's assuming he's home."

"Why don't you call him?"

Cece shrugged. "He doesn't have a cell phone if you can believe that. He's always in his yard mucking about so the only way to contact him is to go over there and hope you can find him and identify yourself before he shoots you as an intruder!"

"What are you talking about?" George's face crumpled into a frown. "Is he really that odd?"

"Oh, probably not. I'm exaggerating. He's seems pretty nice once you get to talking. But I do want Heidi to go with me. That's silly. But it's nice to have company."

CHAPTER TWENTY-SEVEN

Cece drove by Heidi's house and went in. They called the Southwest Wildlife Center. The vets had assessed the ocelot's wounded paw and stabilized it. They predicted a complete recovery and in the meantime mother and babies were doing well.

"Let's head to Fred's house before it rains," Cece commented, glancing up at a darkening sky.

As Heidi climbed in the car, she exclaimed, "Are we really going to drive, what three, four blocks?"

"I know. It seems silly but something tells me I want my car nearby."

"That sounds ominous. Maybe we shouldn't go. It's not like Fred won't find out soon enough. I think he volunteers every week. So he's going to hear about it."

"I know but I just think we should tell him in person."

"Ok, I'm game if you are. Hope we beat the rain. Let's go."

After the short drive, Cece pulled her car up to the curb at Fred's house. They climbed out and stood on the curb, scanning the yard for some sign of a human being.

"We could ring the bell, you know. Like normal people," Heidi said.

"Okay. Probably a waste of time but why not."

They rang once, twice, waited and waited a little longer.

"Come on, let's try the path to the backyard," Cece said. She glanced up at the darkening sky. "Let's hurry. Rain's been threatening all day and now maybe it will finally happen."

They walked single file along the narrow path skirting the overgrowth that obscured much of the way. A movement ahead brought them to a standstill.

"Fred?" Cece called.

They waited. No movement. Then suddenly a form sprung from the overgrowth, hands clutching fistfuls of weeds.

"Hey, Fred. It's Cece and Heidi. Remember us from the Wildlife Center?"

Fred stared back at them silently, an inscrutable frown crossing his brow.

"We've got news we thought you would want to know. The ocelot has been found and captured by Fish and Game and the Liberty Wildlife people helped them! And you were right, a female and she had kittens! Three!" Heidi added excitedly. "They're okay. The vets have them. They're being transferred to Scottsdale to the Southwest Wildlife Center."

Anger spread across Fred's face turning his lips into a downward curve. "Why are you telling me this? What do I care? It doesn't have anything to do with me. It's none of my business and….it's none of yours either."

"But….but," Cece's voice trailed off. She stared at Fred in total confusion. "But you were so upset about Santucci keeping the ocelot that we thought you'd be glad to hear it was okay," she stammered.

Fred stood up straightening his wiry body and slowly dropping the weeds he was holding. He wiped his dirty hands on his threadbare overalls. He took a step toward them, just as the first large drops of rain splashed down on them.

Heidi instinctively stepped back, tripping over a protruding branch and almost losing her balance. Cece turned to grab her arm, steadying her. "Okay, sorry to have bothered you," she huffed as she righted Heidi. "Got to beat the rain. We'll see you around," she called back toward Fred and lifted a hand in an attempt at a breezy wave.

"Let's go," she whispered to Heidi. Pulling her, she noticed the protruding branch that had snagged Heidi's pants' leg. Except it wasn't a branch but rather a pole. She pulled it free from Heidi's pants but the roped other end was ensnarled in a tumble of plants.

"What's that?" Heidi whispered, scrambling to pull herself away from weeds still stuck to the pole.

"Let's go," Cece urged again and dropped the pole. It was instantly buried under a cover of dense vines. They scrambled down the narrow pathway. She glanced quickly behind them to see Fred starting forward, a strange look of anger—or fear—furrowing his features. What had he seen?

They made it to the car and pulled the doors open, sliding in as fast as they could. The rain was now pelting the car. Cece had left the keys in the ignition so it started immediately and they pulled away from the curb just as Fred appeared around the corner of the house.

"Wait!" His call was swallowed up by the wind and rain as they drove away in the opposite direction. Rain sheeted over the windshield as the wipers thumped madly back and forth.

Heidi looked back. "Should we go back? We should tell

him." She twisted in her seat to stare back at his figure, dimming in the pounding rain.

"Are you kidding? No, he's acting too weird. Better to let him find out on his own. And that pole is a loop for catching animals. That's what the guys from Fish and Game used this morning to catch the ocelot. Rabies control uses them to catch vicious dogs. Anyway it's pouring," she added.

"You think Fred used it on the ocelot?"

"I don't know but remember the bandages he had on his arms last time we went to his house…er his yard?"

"Yeah, but he's a gardener. I'm a gardener, you're a gardener. We're always scratched up. Right?"

"True," Cece conceded. "But if Fred used the loop at Santucci's house to try to capture her, he might have been confronted by Santucci and then you know what could have happened."

"Ohhh." They looked at each other and blinked.

"The rope on the loop would have ocelot fur on it if he had used it to catch it. Right?" Cece looked over at Heidi.

"He could have used it on another ocelot maybe."

Cece frowned. "Like the wild ocelot spotted in the Huachucas?"

"Yeah. Why not?"

"Because," Cece answered, "that ocelot was spotted on a camera, not captured. Not to mention that it was on the Mexican border about 300 miles away from here. So that's why not."

Heidi sighed. "Right." She brightened. "But if Fred used that loop to capture Santucci's ocelot, that proves he was at Santucci's house the night of the murder. That's evidence that makes him a suspect."

"And, a loop like that is a kind of *garrot,* isn't it?" Cece turned to Heidi. "What if Dahlia saw Fred there and filmed him. Then she tried to blackmail him with her video and he used it on her and then staged it to look like suicide."

"Holy crap!" Heidi stared at Cece, eyes wide. "That could be the murder weapon, not of Santucci but of Dahlia. That could prove what happened!"

"I…I don't know. It's a lot to assume. It might be the murder weapon. But we don't have it. It's back there."

They had reached the front of Heidi's house and Cece parked on the curb.

"Should we tell the police?"

"Why? They've closed the case. And anyway if Fred saw us picking up the loop, he will be sure to get rid of it. So the evidence would be gone."

"Do you think he saw us with the loop?"

"I don't know. I was way too frantic to get out of there. But it had just started to rain and that might have caught his attention so he didn't see us."

"Maybe."

They sat in the car an extra few minutes before Cece said, "We have to go back and get it."

Heidi started and squeaked out, "What? Now?"

"No, not now. Let's wait a bit. Fred has to go inside at some point. Besides it's still raining. Let's go in your house and wait a half hour or so and then we'll go back."

Cece texted George that she was having a drink at Heidi's house before coming home.

Heidi's husband Hector was engrossed in a basketball game. After a quick hello to him, Cece and Heidi disappeared into the kitchen for a quick glass of wine.

"Fortification," she said. "Just one. Don't want to be woozy or anything." Heidi opened the refrigerator and pulled out a bottle of pinot grigio. She poured the two glasses and they clinked a toast. "To sleuthing," they said simultaneously.

The rain had eased off as they finally pulled their jackets back on and returned to the car. The quick drive of a few blocks to Fred's yard was carried out in silence.

"Should we really do this?" Cece looked over at Heidi.

"Yes? Maybe?"

"Let's not think about it. It will only take a second. We will either find it or not. And the path where it was is just feet from the curb. If we see Fred we'll just drive on. But even Fred must go inside when it gets dark and rains."

"You'd think!"

Cece pulled up to the curb close to the location where she remembered they had stumbled onto the pole. "Let me go," she said.

Before Heidi could respond, Cece had opened the door and jumped out. The tangle of plants glistened in the lamplight. The rain had stopped but everything was soggy and wet. In three leaps, Cece had cleared the plants. Her foot stubbed against the pole. Quickly she pulled it from the undergrowth, and without bothering to clean it off, dragged it back to the car and threw it through the open door into the back seat.

She jumped in, shutting the door as quietly as she could and shifted out of park. The car glided away soundlessly without so much as a noise of protest from Fred's yard.

"Success," crowed Cece. They looked at each other. "Now what?"

"Okay, Cece. I'll take it home and hide it in my house. We'll contact the other clubbers and have a meeting here tomorrow. This should be a group decision."

CHAPTER TWENTY-EIGHT

The clubbers met at Heidi's the next evening. Her house was one of the imposing Tudors with a high pitched pointed roof and elaborate wood trim against pale stucco. The double front door was open as the ladies convened in the living room. Drinks and snacks were arrayed on the coffee table. As everyone settled in, Cece reached down to the floor beside her chair and produced the loop.

She held it up to puzzled frowns. "Huh. What's that?"

Heidi explained their adventure of the night before. They looked at each other quietly.

Stephanie, always the voice of reason, broke the silence. "If Fred is involved in the theft of the ocelot, he could also have been involved in some kind of altercation with Santucci. We know Santucci was at his house that night and he was outside much of the time because of his pool party. He could have seen Fred breaking into the ocelot's cage. The question is this, did Fred fight with Santucci? Did he murder him?"

Stacey jumped in. "If he's guilty of something….theft…not to mention murder and he knows we have evidence against him, then I think he could come after us. At least to get the loop back."

"So what should we do?" Cece asked the group. "Should we turn it over to the police as possible evidence of a crime at the Santucci house, either the breaking and entering to steal a valuable animal or involvement in a murder? Or should we stay out of it for lack of any solid evidence of a crime?"

"It's the police's job to decide if there's enough evidence to investigate what happened as a crime. Right?"

"Let's vote." Cece turned to Heidi. "What's your vote?"

"Let's take it to the police." Heidi told them that she had worried about it all night and wanted to be rid of it. "So what if the police don't care. They've already closed the case and they'll probably think we're just a bunch of snoopy ladies with too much time on our hands. But it is evidence and I don't think we have the right to keep it to ourselves."

"That's their problem. I agree with Heidi. Let's take it in to the city tomorrow so we don't have to worry about it any more." Stacey nodded and turned to Stephanie, eyebrows raised.

"I'm not so sure." Stephanie pulled on a lock of her long hair, twisting it around her forefinger. "I think it's pretty likely that Fred Spencer was at Santucci's house the night of his death. There's no reason to think Santucci would have released his own ocelot and Fred was known to ardently, even violently, object to the way the ocelot was housed. But remember, Heidi, when your son was there around midnight and saw the ocelot loose in the tree, Santucci was very much alive and some of the club girls were still there and Dahlia as well was on the property probably hidden. So I don't think there's any way Fred could have had anything to do with Santucci's death."

Heidi nodded. "Right, of course! Fred might have illegally released the ocelot but he couldn't have murdered Santucci!"

"Unless he went back later." Cece added.

"Noooo. Unlikely." Agreement on that.

"So because of that," Stephanie continued, "I don't think we should try to implicate Fred in this whole affair. So I say no to the police."

"Anne? What do you say?"

She sighed. "I also vote no. Not sure why but maybe we're butting in too much. The police aren't doing a stellar job as we know so I think it's up to us to decide if it's important or not. Let's leave the police out of it because I don't think Fred could have committed the murder—if it is that."

"That leaves me." Cece shifted in her chair uncomfortably. "I'm not sure either but I've seen the crazed look in Fred Spencer's eyes and that memory makes me really, really nervous. So I say the police. I don't want that pole anywhere near me."

"That's three to two to go to the police." Stephanie frowned. "But I have an idea. What if we go to the police with the loop but don't say where it came from. If they question us then I guess we'll have to say. But leave the ball in their court. That way we're giving the evidence to the police but not pointing the finger at any specific person. If the police want to investigate more, they can do it."

"Brilliant!" Cece looked at the others and all smiled in agreement. After a pause, she added, "Let's hope they don't ask us any questions. Not sure they like our being involved so they might just want to brush us off."

"Ha! Likely!" Cece snorted. "So that's decided. Now who is going to take it in? Any volunteers?" She looked around to a lot of shuffling feet and downward stares.

"Oh, okay, you bunch of sissies. I'll do it," Maddie said with a shrug. "I'm at City Hall anyway so I can run it over at lunch time."

"Yay, Maddie." There was an audible sigh of relief and some hand claps.

"Just to recap," Cece said. "I think it's a good idea to go over what we know so far. We now know for sure that Dahlia was at Santucci's that night and possibly at the time of the murder and could have been responsible for his death. We're pretty sure that Fred Spencer was also there and it's much less likely that he could have been responsible for his death. But then Dahlia dies. Dahlia was also possibly murdered and posed to make it look like a suicide. If that happened who had a motive to murder Dahlia? Obviously Fred would if she had seen him fighting with Santucci. And remember we told you about the funeral where it was obvious that Dahlia had at least one serious enemy linked to her relationship with Santucci. So maybe an unknown person would have a motive to murder her."

Heidi joined in. "Remember also that Dahlia was trying to prove she had a relationship with Santucci that entitled her to some kind of ownership to his house. She claimed she had proof that she still owned some of the land the house was built on. What if she could in fact prove that? Then she might be due some kind of inheritance after his death. That gives her a motive to want him dead but it also gives any other heir that might be around a motive to get rid of Dahlia to avoid splitting up the inheritance."

They discussed that issue for awhile without feeling confident they had made headway in resolving the confusion.

"The mansion is worth at least four million," Heidi added. "It would obviously be worth even more if it were in a different neighborhood, like Paradise Valley. In Encanto-Palmcroft, it's an anomaly, a sore thumb. That lessens its value but still, it's worth a bundle. Enough to kill for."

"Don't forget his Scottsdale club and his property or properties in Vegas. The guy's a multimillionaire and then some," Stephanie added.

"What about his daughter Morgan?" Stephanie asked. "At least she has an attorney now so it will probably take some time to establish her position relative to his estate. And remember at the time both Santucci and Dahlia were murdered, if they were, no one but Dahlia knew about the existence of Santucci's daughter or that he even had a daughter."

They all nodded.

"One last thought. The thing that is the most troubling about all this is the fact that Dahlia's phone is missing. We all know she was practically glued to her phone. We know she had it when she snuck into Santucci's backyard on the night before the home tour. She not only had it, she was using it for some purpose that she saw as important. Why else did she go into the gate secretly videoing the party that was going on. But there was no phone when the police searched her house and the shed where she was hung. That makes no sense. I can't help but feel her phone holds the answers to all our questions.

They broke up for the evening agreeing to keep in touch to follow up on the latest happenings. Maddie promised to get back to them about the police response to the loop.

Heidi's parting words to Cece were, "Would you feel a little guilty ratting out Fred Spencer? After all, the ocelot has been found and is safe and Fred was just concerned for its well-being like the rest of us."

"Yeah, I would. I hope it doesn't come to that," Cece admitted. "I just wish he wasn't so scary.

CHAPTER TWENTY-NINE

"Guess what?" Maddie texted everyone the next afternoon. "The police totally blew me off! They said they'd look into it as they took the loop but you could almost see Fotinus rolling his eyes at his partner like we were just a bunch of screwy ladies. Then on top of that he gave me the big once over like I was just there to flirt with him. Ugh."

Cece was sitting in the living room scrolling through her phone when Maddie's text came through. After reading it she called out to George in his study across the hall. "The pole and loop that might have been used on the ocelot when it escaped was found." She hadn't filled in George on the adventures of the night before.

"Really? So someone didn't just open the cage door and let it out?"

Cece got up and walked into the study. "Apparently not. There's evidence that someone might have attempted to not only let the ocelot out of its cage but to move it somewhere else."

George looked up and set his pencil down on the blueprints spread on his drafting table. "So it wasn't just released, someone was trying to steal it."

"Right. And obviously failed since it was seen that very night in a tree outside of Santucci's back wall. But it appears the police are no longer interested in the case. I guess because the ocelot has been captured and Santucci is no longer alive to file a report against the thief."

"All's well that ends well?" George picked his pencil back up and tapped it against the board.

Cece walked by George and plopped down into a spare chair by the window. "Hardly ending well, in my opinion. Two people are dead, a young woman just discovers her birth mother only to lose her after just one meeting and maybe there's a murderer lurking around the neighborhood. The homeless camps, the alien alleys with their night predators, brrrrrr!" Cece shuddered, pulling her sweater a little closer around her shoulders and glancing out the window overlooking the street. After a pause she added, "So what's going to happen to Mar-a-Lago on the Circle? Do you think Morgan has even a chance of getting it?"

"Hard to know. There could be a slew of babies that Santucci produced over the years. It'll take a while to see what shakes out but I wouldn't be surprised if she gets something. What will determine that is if there's a will or a trust. So far there's been no mention of any such document. But we're not really in on any of it. Eventually Morgan will know. If Santucci wasn't married, there is no spouse to get a share. In that case the estate would be evenly divided among any children he might have. Nothing says he has to leave money or anything to his children. It's only if he dies intestate, with no will, that the money is disbursed that way."

Cece thought about that for a moment. "If Santucci was married, he did a good job of hiding it. No wife was ever seen in the short time he lived in that grotesque house. And I think Dahlia would have known it if he was married. No grieving widow or even ex-wife showed up at his funeral."

"She'd probably know. She seemed to be in his face all the time."

"Yeah! He would have been the likely suspect in her death if he hadn't already been dead himself!"

"Ha! Right!"

Cece looked at her watch. Three fifteen. She hoisted herself out of the chair and walked into the hall. "I've been sitting around all day, George. I'm going for a walk. Nicky would love to get out and it's a beautiful afternoon. I think I'm going to poke around in the alley all along that block behind Santucci's house. I'm not at all sure the police did a very thorough search. At the time they searched the area, no one knew that Dahlia had been back there that night so they had little reason to focus on that area. I still can't get over the issue of the missing cell phone."

"I thought you didn't like the alleys." George skewed an eyebrow at her.

"I don't. But only because they're dirty. A lot of weeds and even trash although most people do try to take care of the alleys near their yards. Stacey's daughter says some of the neighborhood kids have build little hideouts in some of the places that have a lot of overgrown bushes and vines. Little secret hideaways."

"Sounds like they're up to no good," George commented.

"I don't think so. Didn't you build forts and try to find little hideaways when you were a kid?"

"Actually, yeah. I did. They were never very successful but we were always trying to find our own secret places. I think most of today's kids can't get off their cell phones long enough to do the kinds of things we did as kids."

Cece lifted Nicky's harness and leash off the coat rack and almost stumbled over Nicky who was there before she even realized he knew exactly what was coming. He squirmed in delight, circling and huffing so furiously that Cece had to tell him to calm down so she could get him hooked up.

"Crock pot's on. Let me get a sweater and a scarf. I'll be back in an hour or so," she called over her shoulder. "Come on, big boy," she urged totally unnecessarily, opening the front door and emerging onto the sunlit patio. Nicky was pulling against his leash in anticipation. "Slow down, will you."

Cece pulled on her sweater and tied a scarf around her chin as a light but chilly wind blew through the palm trees. She headed north along Thirteen Avenue toward the big houses of Encanto. There were few people out on a Wednesday afternoon. The dog walkers tended to be out earlier in the morning or in the evening after work or after dinner, especially now when the days were getting longer. Cece enjoyed the quiet of the neighborhood. There were very few cars on the streets. The presence of the circles effectively discouraged cut through traffic. The design of the neighborhood had been based on a concept called the City Beautiful, a somewhat romantic notion of a tranquil life like one might imagine in a prosperous little English village of a century ago. And if anything in booming new Phoenix resembled that in any way, it was surely here in Encanto-Palmcroft.

After five or six long blocks, Cece and Nicky reached the long alley that bisected the large irregular block where the Santucci house had been built. As they entered the alley the world of manicured lawns and tended flower beds faded away. The alley path was paved in broken cement and lined with overgrown saplings and tall weeds that seemed to close in around them. Although the alley had to be wide enough for city garbage trucks, the canopy of backyard trees in some places totally covered the alley. The spring rains had produced an explosion of weeds reaching three to four feet high along the block walls that separated the backyards from the alley. Cluttering the dense overgrowth were the remnants of trash blowing from the garbage containers as they were upended by the city trucks.

Nicky was beside himself with the multitude of new smells. He was familiar with the smells of the neighborhood dogs that peed with great regularity along the lamp posts and palm tree trunks that lined the streets of Palmcroft and Encanto. Ah, but these smells? Distinctly more catlike, more feral, like the alley itself. This was not the place of his neighboring dogs, no, this was an alien place. Maybe this is where those people that ate the dogs lived. Those ha…. Hay…. Something. Maybe it was ha-haters. He remembered hearing about those unknown dog eaters. That's why there were no dog smells in the alley. Maybe they had all been eaten! What a horrifying thought!. His little furry body was trembling with the notion. He was now a bundle of nervous energy, peeing on every rock and weed within reach until he had not an ounce of pee left in him.

After a half a block the alley turned sharply to the east and joined the east west alley that paralleled Encanto Drive. Cece slowed as they neared the back of the Santucci estate. She peered into the weeds, pushing little troughs through the plants with the toe of her tennis shoe. She was glad the phone she was looking for had such a bright case. That would make it easier to spot. They rounded the corner and progressed to the east zigzagging back and forth across the alley to cover both sides. So far nothing of interest had shown up.

Nearer to Santucci's yard she spotted a pink pile of something very lacy. She poked a toe into the pile and lifted a thong. Jeez, she thought. Were the strippers at the party in the alley? How on earth did such a thing end up in the bushes? Maybe better not to contemplate that for too long. Cece smiled to herself. Maybe she was an old prude after all. Should she pick it up? Evidence? No, of course not. Ick. She kept moving, eyes fixed on the overgrowth snaking up the block walls that separated the yards from the alley. She passed Santucci's property and peered at the tree branches spreading into the alley from his yard. That was where the ocelot had been perched, she thought. And the thin tree that Ryan had pushed himself up in was still leaning against the wall that closed off the view of the swimming pool on the other side. She wondered if he had ever gone ahead and showed his video of the pool party to his friends. She smiled to herself. Probably. She thought Heidi had said that he did. She was just as sure he didn't post anything on the internet. Fontinus had warned him about that. Slowly she made her way toward the far sidewalk and street at the end of the alley.

Nicky was so absorbed in the strange wild cat smells in the alley that when the loud clank sounded behind him, it took a moment for it to register. The loud clank followed by a creak caught them both by surprise. Nicky froze, a deep low growl rumbling in his throat. Cece's breath caught and her chest tightened.

CHAPTER THIRTY

Cece turned to see a gate opening and a large trash container being pushed out. She relaxed, her breath huffing out in relief. How silly she was, she thought. It's an alley in broad daylight in her own neighborhood and she was acting like she was in some sort of enemy territory ready to be assaulted!

Behind the trash can, the lanky arms of a man in a plaid flannel shirt and heavy leather gardening gloves appeared, soon followed by the owlish face of the iris hybridizer.

"Mr. Mortimer," Cece exclaimed, throwing her arms across her chest in relief. "You startled me."

He looked equally startled, staring at her with the same owlish round eyes, magnified by thick round black-wired glasses. He twisted his lips as if to speak but simply looked at her with raised brows.

"I'm Cece," she added quickly, noting his seeming confusion. "Remember me? I was at your talk at the garden center when you spoke so very eloquently about your new iris creations. I said I definitely wanted to select some for my own garden." She felt she was nervously running on at the mouth. "And here you are!! I've been planning on coming by to make my selections before they all faded away."

"Yes." He nodded, she supposed in agreement. "In the alley? You've come to see my flowers?"

"Er, well," Cece stuttered. "Nicky," she nodded down at Nicky who was standing rigidly staring at Mortimer. "He likes to walk in the alleys. Very exciting for a dog, I guess." She gave a nervous little laugh and then added, "Well, since I'm here, what about now? Would that be okay? It will only take a minute and I'll be out of your hair."

Stanley Mortimer looked down at Nicky who was so stiff a whiff of wind would have toppled him.

Cece, following the direction of his eyes, blurted out. "Nicky's no trouble. Such a little thing." She was definitely babbling. Why was this odd man so quiet? Then she remembered how socially anxious he had seemed at the presentation he had made at the garden club and how he had loosened up when he started showing the pictures of his iris.

"Yes," he said again. He pushed his trash container out to its position in the alley and then turned to usher Cece and Nicky through his gate.

"I didn't realize you live so close to the Santucci property. Just the other side of the alley. Not far at all."

Stanley kept walking. "Yes, but I never see him. I don't even know what he looks like. He doesn't take out his own trash," he said, looking her way but not quite looking at her.

"Right, of course not." Cece nodded.

They passed the enclosure that had held the trash container and then the larger backyard opened up before them. It was a fantasy land of iris beds, most still in magnificent bloom. Cece's breath caught. "It's so beautiful," she whispered, fully awed by the sight in front of her.

"I hardly know where to begin." She pulled Nicky along the garden path between the beds of iris. He dug in his front paws until Cece gave a sharp tug on his leash. She was not pleased with him, he knew but it was just so much to take in. The cat smell was even stronger in the yard, especially in the flower beds themselves. Nicky pulled to get a closer sniff but Cece was ignoring him. He knew what to do about the enemy cat smell. Cover it with his scent. That'll show who's the boss!

Cece exclaimed over a beautiful peach hued bearded iris, pointing to it. "That one. I'll take three rhizomes of that one."

Cece looked over the yard and spotted the fabulous Lady Lorraine that Stanley had featured so proudly to the garden club members. She turned to head in that direction but Stanley caught her am. "Over here." He nudged her in a different direction toward the dutch iris beds.

She pulled back. "Yes, they are very beautiful, but I just must have your most glorious creation, the Lady Lorraine. And I think it's such a wonderful tribute to your wife. We're all touched by your dedication to create such a thing of beauty in her honor!"

Cece looked up at Stanley. He was taller than she remembered. But he still had the look of an understuffed scarecrow with an oddly turning head as if he wasn't quite sure where he was looking. But it was the magnified pale blue eyes that stared out over a beaklike nose that produced the image of a raptor, a puffed up hawk watching for an unsuspecting mouse. She inadvertently shrank within herself, stepping back a pace.

She blinked and snapped herself back into the moment. Stanley had reached into the back pocket of his jeans and produced a pencil and a note pad that he flipped open to an empty page.

"I'll write down your order." He looked at her expectantly, pencil posed. He wrote down the peach bearded iris order and looked up again, waiting. Cece named several more varieties and added the number she wanted of each. Stanley carefully recorded the order on his note pad.

Cece turned toward the bed with the Lady Lorraine and started to speak when she realized that Nicky had pulled away from her and was peeing in the very bed they had turned to. Cece froze in horror. "Nooooo, Nicky. Oh my gosh, nooooooo." But it was too late as nature took its turn and next Nicky produced a large poop squarely in the iris bed next to the long green spires of the Lady Lorraine.

"I'm so sorry…." She stammered and turned to Stanley but gulped down the rest of her apology as she watched his face transform into a mask of rage. "Oh-h-h."

Nicky's back legs kicked up a cloud of dirt to cover his business. Again his little rat hunting terrier legs dug into the soft garden soil to fling clods of compost into the air.

Both Cece and Stanley stood transfixed as they stared at the garden bed where a bright yellow object poked up through the trough of misplaced soil. The late afternoon sun sparkled through the hedges to light up the slick plastic surface only partially smeared with the soil it had been buried in.

"Oh-h-h-h!" Cece exhaled again, recognition flooding her brain. The cell phone! Dahlia's cell phone here buried in Stanley Mortimer's backyard. She leaned forward to pluck it from the dirt. Strong fingers wrapped around her arm and yanked her back. The motion caught her off balance and she tottered, dropping Nicky's leash.

Nicky heard Cece's cry of fear and looked up, and seeing

Stanley's action, growled a low and ominous growl.

"Go, Nicky. Run! Run! Home!" Her throat restricted and only a raspy croak broke out of her mouth. But it was enough to snap Nicky's fixation on Stanley's large bobbing Adam's apple and he jerked his head to look into her eyes.

Run, run, what was it? No, it was like walk, a word he knew well. Run—it was like walk but fast. Usually fast, like fun chasing but Nicky understood the sheer terror in Cece's voice and on her face. He knew fear far better than most two-leggeds ever could. It was built into his DNA.

Nicky ran.

CHAPTER THIRTY-ONE

"Oh, Lorraine, don't be upset. I'm here. I'm always here for you. You should have known that before. You didn't really want to go. But it's okay now. I've forgotten all about that bad time. See!" He peered at Cece. His pale blue eyes glittered from beneath virtually lashless lids. The thick lens of his glasses magnified his pupils to owlish proportions. His lips twisted into a grotesque smile, as he slowly nodded his head.

Cece stood frozen, staring into his face, horrified. Lorraine? she thought. His wife, the dead wife?

Stanley blinked rapidly. As Cece's mouth opened to let out a terrified scream, he snapped a hand over her mouth. "You're just upset," he crooned. "I understand. It's been a long day and I know you want a nice cup of tea. We'll just go inside and everything will be fine." His voice was soft and dreamy, his words spreading like a fog obliterating reality. He pulled her toward the house.

She struggled against his force but his loose limbed lanky body was stronger than she would have guessed. Was he insane, in some sort of dissociative state? Clearly he thought she was his wife. What to do? Her thoughts flew around her head as if she had been sucked into a vortex.

"Don't worry about that little dog. Probably lives down the street. Just got lost. He'll go home and be fine. Come, dear. Be by my side."

Nicky had turned back to the alley, the way they had entered the yard. The gate was ajar and he slipped through it, the leash flapping behind him. It wasn't hard for him to backtrack to the south toward their house. Even though he was not familiar with the alley, he could follow their scent. Plus, he knew the way by memory and instinct.

It was late in the afternoon on a lazy spring day. The dog walkers were still not out and the commuters were still not returning home, not for another hour or two, as Cece had noted earlier. The neighborhood was quiet and Nicky ran down the middle of the street toward the triangles, where one street intersected a large grassy diamond shaped park to create two triangles of grass and plants. He jumped over the curb to shortcut across the park when a sudden yank snapped his collar against his throat. His movement stopped midair, his body twisting in response as it fell to the ground.

Scrambling to his feet, he looked back trying to understand what had happened. A low branch protruding from an untrimmed hedge had caught the looped end of the leash. He pulled against the branch until it bent. It did not break. He pulled again, harder but no luck. In a panic, he sat panting and trying to think. Home. Yes, he knew where it was but he could not move. He let out a high pitched howl of despair.

He frantically searched in all directions until he saw movement far down the street that joined the triangles to Encanto Park. A dot was growing bigger. Bigger still. He stood trembling with anticipation. It was a bicycle. As it grew closer he saw it was being ridden by a smallish girl. He recognized her but was not sure who she was. Just a familiar face. He jumped up and down, twisting against the taut leash, barking furiously.

Ollie B pulled up. "Do I know you?" she asked. "Whoever you are, you are really caught, aren't you?" She jumped off her bike, pushed down the kickstand and came over to Nicky. "Hold still." She pulled at his leash to gain some slack and untangled the leash from the branch. "There you go."

She reached for Nicky's collar where she found his dog tag with his name and phone number on one side and address on the other. "Ahh. Nicky. Yes, I think I've met you before. I'll call your owner to let them know you're okay." Still holding the leash despite Nicky's yanking and barking, she pulled her phone out of the backpack that she had placed on the ground next to them. "Be still," she scolded gently. "Let me see the number."

Nicky quieted. Ollie B punched in the number and listened as it rang and rang. No one answered. The recorded voice left instructions and Ollie B replied, "I have Nicky. I found him with his leash caught in the branches at the triangles. I'm going to bring him home to you right now. I'm on my bike."

She closed her phone and placed it back in her backpack. Lifting Nicky's leash and looking down at him, she asked, "Can you run along beside me without me running over you?"

Nicky looked up, trembling with wanting to run as fast as he could but thinking he needed Ollie B to go with him.

She climbed back on her bike and pulled the leash so that

Nicky could run by her side as she pedaled. Nicky had never run beside a bike before and it seemed a little scary but he needed to get home and if this was the way to do it, he would do it!

Off they went heading south on Ninth Avenue to Palm Lane and west to Eleventh Avenue and south again to Coronado and the Palmcroft Way circle. Nicky ran like he had never run before. No stopping for sniffing and peeing. Home! He wanted home!

CHAPTER THIRTY-TWO

George was just pulling into the driveway from a grocery shopping trip when Ollie B and Nicky rounded the curve of the circle. Ollie B hit the brakes and skidded to a stop at the edge of the driveway.

"Whoa, what's this?" George blurted out as he spotted the bike with Nicky beside it.

"Hi, Mr. Coors." Ollie B had read the name on Nicky's tag. "I found Nicky stuck in some branches at the triangles. I tried calling but no one answered so I thought I should just bring him home."

"Oh my," George exclaimed. "How did that happen?"

"I don't know. I just rode my bike by there and I saw him. He was barking like a crazy dog!"

Nicky jumped on George's leg as he turned to close the car door. He was panting so hard he could hardly make a noise but he tried desperately to tell George what had happened.

George stooped down to pat Nicky's head. "It's okay, boy. You're okay."

Nicky was twisting and turning and jumping frantically.

George stood back suddenly, jerking Nicky as well as himself.

"Where's Cece?" He asked, his voice rising with alarm. "Why are you loose? Something has happened." He pulled out his cell phone and dialed Cece's number. It rang and rang. "This is not good," he muttered, his face wrinkling into a mask of worry.

He turned to Ollie B. "Thank you so much for bringing Nicky home. But I'm afraid I need to find Cece. Nicky shouldn't be loose like this. It means something has happened and I need to find out right now."

Ollie B climbed back on her bike and peddled away. She called back, "I hope everything's okay."

"I'm sure it is but I'm going now." George was not the slightest bit sure everything was okay. Cece said she was going to search the alley near Santucci's house so that was where he was going first. Should I call the police? he thought. No, that would make Cece furious and embarrassed. She had probably just stopped, talking to a neighbor. She was notorious for doing that in George's opinion.

"Hop in, Nicky. Let's go!" The thought niggled, if everything was okay and Cece was just chatting somewhere, why didn't she answer her phone and why on earth would she let Nicky go and not be hysterically trying to find him. No, this was not good.

He raced across the streets heading north, ignoring the twenty-five mile an hour speed limit. In minutes he was at the entrance of the alley that ran behind Santucci's house. He drove in. There was nothing. No people, no cars, nothing. He drove the length of the alley and turned around and entered again from the opposite end. He drove slowly but again, nothing. He located the back gate leading into Santucci's yard but nothing was out of place. No sign of anyone or anything.

Nicky jumped up, paws against the window. When they

passed Stanley Mortimer's back gate he barked furiously.

George pulled the car to a stop. He opened the door and Nicky jumped out before George could even get a leg out. "Hold your horses. I'm coming as fast as I can." He hit the ground and reached for the end of Nicky's leash, catching it just before Nicky shot forward.

Nicky ran to the gate that was still ajar, pulling George behind him. George peered in.

"Cece," he called, his voice catching in his throat. "Cece!" Louder. Nicky was pulling harder, pulling him into the yard. As he passed the fenced off trash area and saw the backyard in full sunlight, he stopped. It was a fantasy land of iris beds. This was definitely the yard of the iris hybridizer. George had forgotten his name but remembered that Cece had said she wanted to go to his yard to pick out some of his iris. But that was not today. Today she was looking for the cell phone in the alley. George thought she might have run into the flower guy and decided to make her selections since she was there.

With that thought in mind he walked through the yard and approached a back door with a small covered porch. George pulled Nicky along. He was still twirling and scratching his legs in the dirt. "Calm down," George chastised. He rapped on the door. Waited. Rapped again. He heard a sound inside and waited as the door slowly opened.

Stanley's head popped out. "Yes?"

"Sorry to be at your back door like this but I was walking in the alley and your gate was open. Anyway I was wondering if my wife Cece Coors might have stopped by. She was interested in ordering some of your iris."

Stanley peered down his beaked noise at George. He was

considerably taller and he hunched his shoulders as if holding up suspenders. He shuffled from one foot to the other, observing George with a stare somehow both intense and vacant. "No, no. I haven't seen any one. Just me and my wife here. Keep to ourselves pretty much."

George cleared his throat. "Okay. Sorry to have bothered you. But if you do see her, tell her to call me."

"Yes." Stanley started to close the door. The edge of the door caught on a blue scarf that lay on the floor just inside the door. Stanley toed it hurriedly out of the way. Nicky pushed forward suddenly barking furiously.

George pulled him back. "So sorry. I think he saw a cat. He goes bonkers over cats. Nicky!" He yanked on the leash. "Stop it!" He turned again to Stanley. "I apologize. Let me get him home."

George pulled Nicky away from the porch as the door closed with a click of the latch. Nicky was squirming furiously and barking at the closed door as George pulled him off the porch. He headed to the path that led to the back gate and the alley. Nicky was still pulling against the leash with all his strength, barking all the while. Suddenly Nicky stopped barking and jumped against George's leg, hopping and pawing at his pants leg. George stooped to push him down, shaking his head in worry. He looked into Nicky's face. And at that moment, he realized just how much was wrong with the last few minutes.

He stood stock still. Me and my wife. Me and my wife. Stanley had no wife. Stanley's wife had died of Covid. Everyone in the neighborhood knew about it because the announcement was made over the neighborhood email. Casseroles, cakes and condolences had ensued. It was a big effort at comforting a neighbor in a time of grief. My God, he thought. And that iris in her honor! He paused, shaking with a memory. That blue thing caught in the door. He saw it in his mind's eye. He had hardly noticed it with Nicky carrying on so crazily. But now that he thought about it, he realized it looked like Cece's scarf. His heart raced with the realization that something horrible had happened.

He turned toward the side yard, threw open the gate and ran to the front of the house as he pulled out his phone and dialed 911. He found the house number by the front door and conveyed the number and street to the dispatcher. He pounded on the front door, yelling, "Open up, open up. I'm coming in." He rattled the door knob and pushed his shoulder against the door. It would not budge.

Nicky joined in the cacophony of noise. George yelled until he was hoarse. He looked around the porch area for a rock or something to throw through a window. He pulled Nicky into a flower bed under a front window that was lined in bricks. He stooped to wrench a brick out of the soil and as he aimed it at the window near the door, he heard a siren wailing. Never had such a sound been more welcoming.

He ran to the sidewalk along the edge of the yard as a police cruiser rounded the curve. Dropping the brick he waved frantically at the approaching car. It pulled to the curb and two officers leapt out. George was screaming and pointing to the house.

The first officer grabbed his arm. "Tell us what has happened."

"He has my wife," George shouted, waving his arm frantically toward the front door.

"Hold on! Hold on!" The officer held him back and both cops strode to the door and pounded. "Police! Open up!"

George pushed up behind one of the cops who held his arm out to block his way.

The cops pounded again and stood back.

The door opened slowly and Stanley peered out, his owlish eyes squinting as the setting sun shone into his face. He blinked and his eyes opened wide. "Thank god you're here. There's a crazy man screaming in my yard. And his vicious dog tried to attack my wife and now he's off the rails saying horrible stuff about me. There they are." He pointed at George standing behind the cops.

"Everybody calm down," the first cop said. "Open the door and come out so we can get this all sorted out."

"No. His dog is rabid. He's a danger!" Stanley pointed at Nicky, opening the door wider to accommodate his broad shoulders.

With a jerk on the leash, Nicky lunged forward, scooting through Stanley's long legs and disappearing into the room beyond.

Stanley screamed, "Stop him! He's attacking! He's a mad dog." His face transformed into a mask of rage. His entire body was shaking. He turned and dove back into the room, trying to catch the flapping end of the leash but it was too late. Nicky was gone.

The cops both pushed past Stanley into the living room. It was empty but a door stood open at the far end of the room. They crossed the room in quick strides and into the room beyond. There was Nicky jumping onto Cece who was tied to a chair with a gag in her mouth.

Stanley froze on the threshold of the room, blinking and muttering. "Leave her alone. She's not well. She has Covid. You have to leave. She's contagious and has to be isolated. You need to leave," he breathed out slowly like a balloon hissing out the last of its air. His body slumped.

The first cop rushed to Cece's side and pulled off her gag. He brought out a pocket knife to cut the cords tying her hands behind her while the second cop gripped Stanley by the arm and pulled him away. Nicky was jumping and yowling frantically. The cop pushed him aside and George ran over to grab his leash. "Oh Cece," he half sobbed as he and Nicky both ran to her side.

As the ropes fell off, Cece stood tentatively rubbing her wrists and stretching her body. She turned to George. "I'm okay. But thank god you got here. Stanley's having some kind of psychotic break. He thinks I'm his wife." George held her and squeezed so hard Cece laughed through her shaking. "I'm okay," she said again and freed herself from George's hug to reach down to pat Nicky's head. "Thanks, little guy. You two are my heroes!"

"We'll need for you to go to the station for a statement," said the officer who had freed Cece.

Cece noticed his name tag. "Thank you, Officer Sanchez. I can't tell you how glad I am to see you." She looked over to Stanley who was being led out of the front door by the other officer. "What's going to happen to him? He's clearly in some kind of dissociative state. He kept saying that I really didn't want to leave him, I just thought I did but he was sure I didn't mean it. I guess he really thought I was his wife. And she was said to have died in California while she was visiting her sick mother."

"We'll find out. He'll be questioned very thoroughly. But for now if you're up to it, we need you to come to the station to give a statement. Do you think you can do that?"

Cece looked at George and nodded her head. "Yes, I can and

I think it's best that I do that while everything is fresh in my head. I have a feeling I'm going to want to forget about this awfulness as quickly as I can."

CHAPTER THIRTY-THREE

George, Cece and Nicky walked around the side yard of Stanley's house and through his beautiful backyard alive with the beautiful blooms of iris. George was gripping her waist which Cece appreciated since she was still feeling a little shaky. She scanned the iris beds as they headed for the back gate. Iris, Cece thought, her eyes sweeping across the vibrantly colored beds. The Greek goddess of the rainbow. How apt. So much beauty yet with such mind bending delusion in the same man who created them. How could they exist in proximity? She took a last look at the beautiful Lady Lorraine and there was the yellow cased cell phone still lying in the dirt where Nicky had dislodged it. She had almost forgotten it in the craziness that she had just been through. Now she walked over and picked it up, brushing off the last smears of dirt.

She turned to George, holding up the phone triumphantly. "This is what it's all about, I'm pretty sure." She nodded. "This is going to the police station!"

The car was still in the alley where George had left it. No one seemed to have noticed it or cared. They climbed in and Nicky jumped onto Cece's lap. Everything was as it should be again.

He was happy.

As soon as they reached their house, George stopped the car and took Nicky inside, leaving Cece waiting in the car. Once in the house he checked to make sure Nicky's water bowl was full and added a quick handful of dog kibble to his food bowl. "Not sure how long we'll be, big boy. But we'll be back as soon as we can."

Nicky knew what that meant. But he was happy nonetheless and jumped up on the pillows on the back of the sofa to take a much needed snooze.

George and Cece drove south on Seventh Avenue to the Washington Street central police station. Once settled into an interrogation room, they were joined by the two detectives who had interviewed them following Santucci's death, Detectives Fotinus and Miller. Cece recounted the entire story of her meeting with Stanley in the alley and how she wanted to order some iris and thought it was a good time to go ahead and do that. The most important part of her story was when Nicky accidentally dug up the cell phone in the yellow plastic case. She pulled the cell phone from her purse and placed it on the table. "This belonged to Dahlia Walker, the woman who was involved with Sal Santucci and later found hung in a shed behind her house. As you know, a witness, a kid from the neighborhood, saw her the night of Santucci's death with this phone secretly videoing a swim party from a hiding place just outside his yard from the alley. Santucci's house and Stanley Mortimer's house are just across the alley from each other. So why did it end up buried in

Stanley Mortimer's backyard flower bed? Dahlia apparently had it at the time of Santucci's death on March sixteenth but when her body was found a week and a half later, the phone was missing. So obviously this is an important part of the explanation of what happened to Sal Santucci!"

"Eh, right." Detective Fotinus looked at his partner. "This is now a whole new ball game." He looked at Cece and George, eyebrows raised. "And just how do you two know about all this?"

George coughed tentatively and held up both hands, palms out. "Not me, Detective." He nodded in Cece's direction. "It's her and her book club. They've been investigating both Santucci's death and Dahlia Walker's death for the last month or more." He folded his arms over his chest and puffed out his cheeks. "Regular private eyes, they are!"

"Are they now?" Detective Fotinus' words were edged with sarcasm and he eyed Cece suspiciously. "Your book club?"

"Yes." Cece sat up a little straighter and smiled sweetly. "We know why Dahlia was at Santucci's house the night of the murder…"

"Whoa, there. Murder? Who said it was a murder?"

"Remember, I'm the one who found Santucci's body in his fish pond on the Sunday of the home tour. So I've been involved from the start whether I wanted to be or not. But my book club got involved because someone dying like that in our neighborhood is something we care a lot about. So we've been doing our own investigation. Sort of parallel to the department's. As you know, the department stopped investigating. But we didn't. So murder, you ask? We say we think it was a murder? We do! That's what we have been trying to determine, exactly what happened. We also are not at all sure that Dahlia's death was a suicide. We think it also could have been a murder. I think the evidence is going to be on that phone. You just need to break into it and see what it reveals."

Detective Fotinus scowled and picked up the phone. He placed into an evidence envelope that Detective Miller produced and turned to Cece. "Yes. We'll see. We'll keep in touch."

George started to rise from his chair. "My wife has just been through a harrowing experience and I think she needs to get home to rest and recover. So if that's all for now, could we leave?"

"I understand. Certainly. We will be back in touch soon and we will need a formal statement."

With that, George and Cece headed for the door. Cece muttered under her breath, "and thank you, ladies." They walked as quickly as they could to the parking lot. "Let's get home," George said. "I know one little furry guy who will be anxiously awaiting us.

Two days later, George and Cece were summoned back to the police station. They sat in the same stuffy interrogation room with Detectives Fotinus and Miller.

"We've broken into the phone," Fotinus started without any chitchat prelude.

Cece's eyes widened. "And?" She looked at the detectives excitedly.

"The video is dark and some of it is from a distance which makes it even less clear but it shows first the pool party and the few girls there in the process of leaving. But there's a gap and then it shows Stanley Mortimer entering the yard. There are snatches of a confrontation. Mr. Mortimer was screaming at Santucci about his ocelot. It had jumped his back wall and was using his iris bed as a cat box. Mortimer was furious and started pushing Santucci who was pretty drunk and not too steady on his feet. Finally he shoved Santucci into his fish pond and sat on him, holding him under water until he drowned. That's what's on the video!"

Cece gasped, "Oh my gosh. So that's what happened. So, of course. Once she had that on tape, she tried to blackmail him! That's what she meant when she told Morgan she was going to come into some money soon."

"Wait, who's Morgan?" Detective Fotinus was taking rapid notes in a pad on the table.

Cece explained how her book clubbers had found the correspondence between Dahlia and the daughter she had given up at birth. And, how Dahlia had wanted to prove that Santucci was Morgan's father. "Maybe Dahlia couldn't get anything from Santucci despite the fact that he had cheated her out of her mother's house but she thought at least she could get something for Morgan. I think she wanted to do something to make up for giving her up for adoption so many years earlier. And that's why she probably wasn't so upset when she found out she had been seen in the alley. Because she knew she had proof to show she had not killed Santucci and she could prove who did. Her only mistake, and it was monumental, was that she didn't turn over the evidence on her phone at that time. She was thinking she could confront Mortimer with the video and get money from him. She way overestimated her power to make that happen."

Detective Fotinus closed his notepad. "Anything else?" He looked to Cece, then George and back to Cece. "No? We'll need a formal statement in a few days so don't leave town."

"But the world tour?" Cece gasped.

"Or for heaven's sake," George laughed. "Don't worry, Detective. She's kidding. No world tour."

"Hummm, quite the joker, aren't you."

"Oh, sorry," Cece smiled sweetly. "But we clubbers were quite helpful, weren't we?"

"Yes, you were."

"You're welcome."

CHAPTER THIRTY-FOUR

Three days later, for the third time, George and Cece sat in the interrogation room.

"Mortimer confessed," Detective Fotinus started abruptly. "He knew we had the evidence that he killed Santucci and he pretty much confessed to murdering Dahlia Walker as well. He said she lured him over to her house pretending to be interested in him but then showed him the video and asked for money to keep quiet about it. He didn't say but I think Mortimer realized that she wouldn't keep quiet no matter what he gave her because then she would be the primary suspect. The only way she could clear herself was by showing the police the video. So he decided he had to shut her up and get rid of the video. He told her he'd give her the money but had to go to the bank to get it. So they arranged to meet the next day. That's when he came up with the idea of strangling her and making it look like a suicide. He thought it would work because everyone knew how much she despised Santucci. So it would look like committing suicide was basically an admission of guilt. Better to die than spend the rest of your life in prison." Fontinus paused a moment before adding, "He seemed enraged that Dahlia had lied to him about wanting a relationship with him. Apparently he thought she was really into him and when he realized she didn't care about him at all but had tricked him, he snapped. 'Just another lying woman,' he kept saying over and over. He wanted vengeance."

"I saw her talking to Mortimer the day before at the Sunday schmooze," Cece interrupted.

Fotinus scowled at her. "Schmooze?"

Cece waved her hand. "Oh, it's a neighborhood social function held every month. Open to everyone. Dahlia was there and so was Stanley Mortimer. I saw them talking together rather animatedly. I bet that's when she set it up for him to meet her at her house."

Detective Fotinus looked at his partner and nodded. "Because of your statements, Ms. Coors, about his calling you his wife like he was in some sort of delusional state, we had reason to believe there might have been foul play involving his wife. We got in touch with the California authorities and discovered that there was no death certificate for a Lorraine Mortimer. Only one for her mother. We found a record of a plane ticket for a Lorraine Mortimer from San Diego to Phoenix on February 16, 2022, and that she had flown back just six days before Stanley Mortimer announced on the neighborhood email that his wife had died in California.

"When he was confronted with all this, he broke down and admitted that he had killed her. Accidentally he said, because she wanted to leave him and go back to California and live in her mother's house. And she didn't want him there. She wanted a divorce. He couldn't let that happen. He said he just wanted to stop her from leaving, not hurt her. He thought he could convince her to stay but she refused to listen. She started screaming at him and he just wanted to stop her screaming. He choked her so she would stop. That's what he said. But he knew what he had done so he buried her in his backyard under the iris bed where he grew her namesake iris." He paused for a moment, clearing his throat and tapping his fingers on the table. "It was the ocelot that started digging up that bed where her body was that made him go berserk the night of the swim party at Santucci's. That's why he went over there in such a fury. And that was the beginning of the end."

"Wow!" Cece looked at George. "He looked too much like a predator hawk not to be one. Despite his nerdy engineer facade."

"The yard and house have been closed off and the excavation of the backyard quickly revealed the remains of Lorraine Mortimer. The forensics lab will verify the identification but it's unlikely to be anything different."

The book clubbers gathered at Cece's the following night. "Champagne everyone," she held up the bottle and popped the cork. It flew across the room and smacked against the door to the backyard.

"Here's to that weasel Mortimer," Stacey held out a wine glass to be filled and lifted it to the ceiling. "Lock him up!"

"He's a vulture, more like it." Cece said. "Anyway, here's to Stanley Mortimer in jail for the rest of his life!"

"Poor Cece. You must have been terrified." Nodding heads all around. "I can't imagine what it must have been like," Stephanie added.

Cece looked around the group. Her friends, she thought.

They were always there for her. And of course the group of them was why she had gotten into so much trouble in the first place. She did it to herself. They all did it. She smiled. It was so worth it. Then she said to them all, "I was pretty scared. I just keep praying that Nicky had run home to George and he would be there and figure out to come looking for me." Cece looked around at Nicky who was in his usual place behind her head on the back pillow of the sofa. "Of course now George says he's lucky he didn't have a heart attack on the spot and die! So much for my being scared." She laughed. "But seriously, he was yelling and banging on the door and I didn't know if Stanley was going to go out and attack him too. So I do feel a little guilty. I don't think George's cardiologist would have approved the whole thing."

"He's tougher than you think, Cece," Anne added. "Thank goodness he could act so quickly."

Cece smiled and nodded. That was certainly true.

"But what about Stanley? What if he pleads insanity?" Heidi asked. "What do you think, Stephanie. You know about this stuff a lot more than the rest of us."

"The insanity defense isn't as easy to pull off as some people think." Stephanie filled her glass and took a sip. She sighed and added, "Isn't everyone who murders someone at least a little crazy? But it sounds like Stanley Mortimer was more than just normal crazy, like anyone who gets mad enough. He was obviously in a delusional dissociative state if he thought Cece was his wife so he might really not have known who she was or what he was doing. But I think he'd have a hard time convincing a jury of that. Especially because he murdered three people and the second murder, Santucci's, was done quite rationally and purposefully. You don't sit on a man under water until he drowns if you're in some kind of whacked out state of mind. And Dahlia's murder was planned and staged very methodically and then he went about like nothing had happened. Despite all that I think it's certainly possible that he has a personality disorder. But that doesn't mean he's crazy, crazy, like psychotic or schizophrenic."

"Like what kind of disorder?" Anne asked. "Like narcissism?"

"A lot of people are narcissists but I don't think they're considered mentally ill."

"They probably should be considered that."

"Ha! Half the population would be locked away."

"That would be weird," Cece added.

"He could have borderline personality disorder or something like that," Stephanie said. "It's a controversial diagnosis but a lot of therapists think it's legitimate. A defining behavior for a BPD person is an inability to accept rejection. They're the stalkers, the ones that after a breakup refuse to leave, keep showing up. Often becoming increasingly desperate to maintain a relationship that's clearly over. Desperate to the point of losing touch with reality. Or like the ones that actually believe they're in a relationship with a movie star or someone famous. Remember the Jodie Foster case? I think that was the one."

"Not sure I remember that." Maddie looked around at the others.

"You're too young," Heidi laughed. "It was a long time ago. Jodie Foster had a stalker who ended up shooting Ronald Reagan in an attempt to prove his love for Jodie. She of course had no idea who he was. How whacked out is that?"

"Remember that movie, Fatal Attraction? That was another

one!"

"The rabbit boiling in the pot! That was so horrible! I still remember that," Stacey added.

"Wow," Maddie exclaimed. "I missed those."

"I should add," interjected Stephanie, "that people with that disorder are usually a bigger danger to themselves than anyone else."

"Why does that not make me feel safer?" Cece sighed. "Anyway, Stanley couldn't accept his wife wanting a divorce. So he snapped when his wife came back from San Diego and said she was leaving him. The only way he could keep her was to kill her. Although he didn't tell it that way," Cece added, remembering the way Detective Fotinus had described the confession.

"One good thing that happened because of all of this was the ocelot." Stacey held up both hands. "Listen up because it's good news for a change. The kids' club kids have kept in touch with Liberty Wildlife Center and they've just learned that the ocelot mama plus her kittens are going to be transferred from Southwest Wildlife to the Phoenix Zoo. So they now have a permanent home and the kittens can stay with their mother for several years as they do in the wild. Or maybe longer."

"That's great!" Cece smiled and sighed. A long journey for the cat lady, she thought. No more tiny cages and cramped living. "I bet Fred is happy!"

"Yeah," Heidi added. "I'm pretty sure that he's the one who released her. If he did, I think now that it's over, he doesn't have to worry any longer."

"That should put a smile on his face. He does seem to be a nice guy despite his rather odd behavior toward us. Probably the result of his feeling guilty and thinking we might find out and turn him in. Plus if he did try to capture the ocelot, he failed and it got loose. So that was even worse. He committed a crime by stealing it and then he made the situation for the ocelot worse, not better. Pretty bad screw up." Heidi shrugged and held up her glass. "To Fred, also, and all the wildlife biologists who keep our world a better place for all living beings. Or at least try!"

They all cheered and clinked their glasses.

"And here's the cherry on top of the whole ocelot episode," Stacey added. "The zoo awarded the kids' club the privilege of naming her. Guess what they chose?" She looked around at their blank faces. "Cat Lady! Cat Lady with Children!"

"The zoo let them do that?"

"Yep. They did!" They all laughed and cheered.

"Not to change the subject but let's think about Morgan for a minute. She needs to know about all of this and I think we should tell her before it shows up in the newspapers and social media," Anne said.

"Yes, what about Morgan?" they all chorused.

"I'll call her first thing tomorrow and see if we can meet up. What do you all think about going to the Egyptian?"

They all thought that was a great idea. "Text us if you get a time and day. We need to tell her privately. It's good news in many ways but none of this is easy for Morgan."

"Right. Her life has been turned upside down. But just think, she may be rich after all. I want to know the status of Santucci's estate."

Thursday Anne texted everyone. Friday at five. Courtyard at the Egyptian.

When they all gathered on Friday, husbands in tow, they settled into a circle of chairs in the open air seating area. The ladies got up and walked around the back of the stage and down the row of motel rooms to the airstream trailer where they saw Morgan and Vincent talking with their band members. Morgan greeted them warmly. "What's going on?" she asked, looking at them expectantly.

"We have news about your mother," Anne started. Then she told Morgan the whole story of her mother's murder.

At the end, Morgan sighed. "She took an awful risk to try to get money for me. I just wish I had known. I would have kept her from doing it but she didn't tell me. I guess she knew enough to hide blackmail. But in her own misguided way she was thinking about me and wanting to help me. I will be always grateful to know that. She wanted to know me and not give up. Knowing that it was not a suicide makes me have more peace with what happened, horrible as it was."

Cece nodded sympathetically.

"How's your claim going with your lawyers?" Maddie asked. "Do you have Meredith Bigley, I hope?" Maddie was the one who had steered Morgan to legal representation after the paternity was established.

"Good," Morgan answered. "And thanks for giving me her name. She's great and has a fabulous reputation. Plus I like her a lot. So far only one other person has come out of the woodwork claiming to be an heir and Meredith is pretty sure his claim is spurious. But it's going to take awhile. Maybe a year."

"What about his house?" Cece asked.

"It's closed up. One of his club managers is making sure it's all right. They're taking care of everything, the two clubs and the house. Obviously I'm not in a position to have any say in any of it yet. But," she added, "when it's all settled and if I inherit it, I'm going to sell the club in Vegas and turn the Scottsdale club into a music venue. Vincent and I are pretty excited about it. We don't know for sure what we'll do with his house. It's much too big for us but at least for the near future we'll be using it to house some of our musician friends. Sort of like a co-op. We'll have to check out the details with the city because of the historic designation but we think we might be able to work out something that will be agreeable to everyone. So much to plan, I hardly know where to start!"

"What!!!" No more strippers?" They all laughed.

"Just when I thought I might give it a try." Stephanie gave a little bootie shake.

"Ha, ha! That's a good one. We'd all have to drag you onto the stage to get you to take off your sweater!"

"Humph. Little do you all know," she snorted.

"That'll be a good one if you do. We'll come to cheer you on," they all agreed.

The rest of the evening was an enjoyable dinner and entertainment. Morgan and Vincent sang together so beautifully it brought tears to Cece's eyes. Morgan sang again the song she wrote in her mother's honor. They were all near tears. When they left, they all agreed to keep in touch. As Cece and George drove home, George took a different route and turned onto Encanto Drive. They crept past the Santucci house and stared at its garish fountain spewing swirls of water toward waiting cupids. George sighed and shook his head. What was there to say?

Nicky greeted them at the door as they turned the key to enter. He jumped up and down with more than his usual enthusiasm, maybe sensing that he would not always know for sure what they were doing and where they would be. George sat down in his favorite chair and picked up the remote. Cece settled onto the sofa and Nicky snuggled up next to her, resting his furry head on her leg. She idly stroked his silky ears. "You're my boy," she murmured.

All's good. We're all home. No cooties here, he thought with a sigh.

EPILOGUE

One year later……

Cece and the book clubbers were seated at a large round table in the side yard of the mansion that had once belonged to Sal Santucci. It was a beautiful March day. Nicky was happily stretched out under Cece's chair.

"What a day for a wedding," Cece smiled and looked around affectionately at her four friends. "And what a day for a happy ending."

"Yeah," Anne said. "Forget about the ides of March. This ides of March is a whole different story."

The Encanto-Palmcroft Books and Bonding clubbers had gathered at the once infamous house to wait for the beginning of the marriage between Morgan Thompson and Vincent Barker. Title to the house had been transferred into Morgan's name just days before the wedding which was a big relief to everyone. It was a small wedding but this was where Morgan wanted it. The guests were just Morgan and Vincent's musician friends who were of course also playing for the wedding and a handful of others. Plus there were a few of the employees from the Santucci clubs that Morgan had befriended.

And now Morgan and Vincent were to be married in the very side yard where it had all started just a year earlier. The pond had been refurbished and the side yard manicured. The outrageous fountain in the front had hurriedly been taken down and a flower garden planted in its place.

"Just think about all that happened just a year ago," Cece said, nodding her head thoughtfully and surveying her group of friends. "Two murders and Stanley Mortimer in prison awaiting sentencing, an imprisoned ocelot with three kittens now happily ensconced at the Phoenix Zoo, and Morgan now the acknowledged heir to the Santucci estate. Plus this architectural misfit now looking much more at home in the neighborhood. And Morgan about to be married!"

"By the way, has anyone seen Fred recently?" Cece asked.

"As a matter of fact I have," Stacey responded. "I took Ollie B to Liberty Wildlife last week and we ran into Fred. He actually was kind of chatty and even had a discussion with Ollie about the American kestrel she saw at the park the other day. They're quite the pair of birders, it seems. Ollie B wants to volunteer there when she's old enough."

"That's great," Stephanie smiled. "I think it really helps kids grow up when they do something for the community at large. Helps keep them grounded and away from constant social media."

They all agreed with that.

"I bet Fred's a lot calmer now that the whole ocelot incident has been resolved so satisfactorily." She paused and added, "Do you think we'll ever know who released Cat Lady?"

"Nope, and just as well!" Stacey said with an emphatic nod.

"And Ryan is beside himself with anticipation of testifying in Stanley's upcoming trial," Heidi added. "He's even saying he's going to enroll in Phoenix College's crime scene investigation classes next year. Don't know how all that will go but it's great to see him focused on his college future. Better than trying for some kind of TikTok fame," she added ruefully.

"So, all's well that ends well."

"Just one unresolved issue." Cece sighed. "Carrie! Our real life cat lady. Where is she and what has happened to her?"

Anne joined in. "The homeless people, er, unhoused people, are gone from the park for now. But for how long? And where are they now? Will there ever be an answer for them?" She shook her head. "Maybe not."

"On a happier note the next home tour is just a year away," Stephanie added with arched eyebrows. "It'll be our big anniversary tour. One hundred years since the founding of Encanto-Palmcroft! I wonder what will happen on that one!"

Their contemplation of that juicy question was interrupted when the side door opened and all looked up as Morgan stepped out of the kitchen door and headed across the lawn to join them. She was radiant in a short white dress with lacy sleeves and neckline. Her lustrous dark curls circled her neck and fell to her shoulders.

"Ten minutes or more and we'll start," she told them. "I just wanted to zip over and say hello. We'll talk more after the ceremony but I had to say thank you to all of you. I can't imagine what would have happened if you all had not cared so much. Thank you all so very, very much."

"Thank you too. Thanks for inviting us to your very special

day. And thanks for including Nicky too." Cece looked up at Morgan shading her eyes from the sun and added brightly, "You look gorgeous!"

"Thank you." She turned to Nicky and reached down to pat his head. Nicky flattened his ears and half closed his eyes, a doggie version of "ahhhh." "He's my hero. He's part of the story too. You all are. I don't think any of this would have happened without all of you."

They all grinned. "It's our neighborhood and we care what happens here. And now you're a part of it too. At least for a while. And nothing could make us happier!" Anne spoke for the group and they nodded agreement.

"And look at all this." Cece waved a hand around the yard. "So beautiful!"

"If you do sell the house, where will you go, Morgan?" Cece asked gently.

Morgan smiled and tilted her head as if imagining all the houses that could be. "We're not sure, but Vincent and I want to buy a house together, one that we both choose. We're looking in Palmcroft so I think we'll still be neighbors."

"That's great."

"But you're here for now and it's absolutely beautiful. The yard is gorgeous!" They all chimed in an agreement.

Morgan smiled. "Thank you all. After Dahlia was cremated, I saved her ashes, waiting for an idea of where they should go, where it would make her the happiest to be. And I finally realized that it was here, here in this house where her own mother's house once stood. So I put the ashes into the soil when the new beds were being dug around the side yard. And now the beds are planted and the bushes are in full bloom just in time for the wedding."

"Yes, yellow bells, how beautiful and how appropriate. Her favorite color. Dahlia would have loved it!"

Nicky barked!

Ginny Barnes has been an author and editor for state and national K-12 textbooks and an instructor at Phoenix College. She holds a PhD in anthropology from Arizona State University. She divides her time between Prescott and Phoenix where she lives with her husband and their miniature schnauzer Nicky. When not writing she enjoys gardening, thrifting, rug hooking and painting (both walls and canvas).

www.ingramcontent.com/pod-product-compliance
Lightning Source LLC
Chambersburg PA
CBHW030134010826